Jessica Watkins Presents

COVERED IN YOUR LOVE 2
The Finale

by **NIQUE LUARKS**

Chapter One

Life Ain't Fair

Nas

Holding Jaime in my arms brought back memories of my little brother taking his last breath. The only difference was my bro wasn't scared to die. The look in Jaime's eyes, though...she was terrified. Even though she was having a hard time keeping them open, I saw how scared she was. I, on the other hand, didn't know how to feel. I was used to death. I dealt with the shit on a daily basis, but seeing Jaime suffer and knowing I couldn't do shit, was putting a nigga in his feelings.

"Hold on, Jaime, a'ight?" I heard sirens getting closer. "Hold on, Ma."

The only reason I hadn't just scooped her up and rushed her to the hospital myself was because I needed to keep her head elevated. I didn't want her to choke on her own blood.

"Meme!" Jade's hoe ass dropped down next to us. "She's dying," she cried loudly, causing Jaime to panic, which pissed me off. I needed Jaime to stay calm. I didn't want her to think she

COVERED IN YOUR LOVE 2
by *Nique Luarks*

was about to check out when that might not even be the case. Running my hands through her soft hair, I pulled her closer to me. I wasn't used to emotions like this; feeling helpless.

"You straight, Jaime," I assured her even though I wasn't sure. "Chill out, Ma." I looked up the street just as the ambulance came zooming down in our direction.

"Jaime, please don't die," Jade begged.

"Shut the fuck up," I addressed Jade with a mean mug.

"This is my sister!" she cried, wiping the snot off of her face.

I didn't give a fuck about all that. If she caused Jaime to panic, it would only send my lil' baby into shock. I couldn't afford that. Duke needed Jaime around more than Jade or me. I didn't need Jade to put extra stress on her.

"Everybody step back!" someone behind me yelled.

I kissed Jaime's forehead just as a medic came to my side.

"How many times was she hit?" he asked as they came with a gurney.

"Shit, once, twice…" The blood on the front of her shirt was now soaking through my clothes.

They lifted Jaime out of my arms, and she started coughing and choking again.

Hold on, baby.

COVERED IN YOUR LOVE 2
by *Nique Luarks*

I watched as they placed her on the gurney and rushed her back to the ambulance. Following close behind them, I checked my surroundings and noticed the block was now crowded. As we reached the ambulance, they ripped Jaime's shirt open, exposing the gunshot wound in her chest.

Fuck.

Anger slowly consumed me as they hooked her up to a machine.

"Her heart rate is slowing! We're losing her!"

"Noooo," Jade whimpered next to me.

"Are you family?" a woman asked, working on Jaime as they got ready to shut the doors.

"Yes, I—"

"Yeah," I cut Jade off. "I'm her husband." Climbing into the ambulance, I took a seat and grabbed Jaime's small, cold hand.

Hold on, Ma. I kissed the back of her hand as they shut the doors.

Ryan

Looking back and forth between Quan and his bitch, it took everything in me to not spazz the fuck out and lose my mind. It was like everything was moving in slow motion. Instead of jumping on him like I wanted, I spun around and practically ran back to Blaze's whip she had let me use for my temporary stay.

"Yo, Ry, wait man," Quan said behind me.

Through blurred vision, I reached the driver's side and fumbled with the handle.

"Ryan." Quan grabbed me roughly by my forearm, spinning me around. "Where you going?" He stared down at me and I broke down into a fit of tears.

Brianna's words cut through my conscience, making me feel sick to my stomach. I needed to get away from her, him...them. Or I would be in jail for murder.

"Ry," he said in a softened voice. "Calm down." Wiping my cheeks with his thumbs, he sighed. "Chill."

"You...how…" I cried harder. "Why would you give her a baby when you know I can't have one?" My shoulders bounced as he pulled me in for a hug.

"I'm sorry," he mumbled into my hair, rocking me slowly.

4

COVERED IN YOUR LOVE 2
by *Nique Luarks*

"You said you loved me," I whimpered. "You said you loved me Quan." We'd been trying to have a baby for years...*years*, but nothing. Now, here he was, the love of my life, giving another woman what I wanted, but couldn't give him. The shit hurt so bad I wanted to slit my wrists and die.

"You know I love you, man." He sighed. "You my world...*My Ry*. I fucked up. I'm sorry, man." He sounded just as defeated as I felt.

"DaQuan we need to—"

"Brianna, take yo ass home, man." He held onto me tighter. "Ryan, stop crying before you make yourself sick, yo."

Stop crying? How could I? Yeah Quan and I were broken up, but Brianna was pregnant and showing, which meant she'd gotten pregnant while we were together. I cried harder. It literally hurt to breathe in. Quan was killing me.

"Stop, baby," he pleaded, placing his lips on my neck.

"I need to go," I managed to get out. "Let me go," I stated coldly, looking off in a daze.

"I ain't letting you drive like this," he shot back, lips still on my neck.

Even though I missed his touch, his scent...*him*. I had to get away from him. Pulling away, I sniffled, avoiding eye contact.

"This is some bullshit!" Brianna spat, storming away.

Quan didn't fully let me go until she got in her car, backed out of the drive way, and pulled off down the street. When he did, he gripped my chin, making me look up at him. I could still see the love in his eyes. I even felt it when he placed his forehead on mine and sighed. We stood there silently until he stepped back and ran his hands down his face in frustration. Opening the driver's door, I took one more look at my everything and got in.

Chapter Two

All Things Go

Jaime

Even though my eyes felt like they were glued shut, I could still hear machines beeping all around me. A small whimper escaped my lips as I tried to open my eyes. Finally, they slowly opened and with fuzzy vision, I looked up at the ceiling. Blinking a few times, I sniffled as warm tears slid down both sides of my face and into my ears.

Taking in a slow, shaky breath, I exhaled slowly, trying to calm myself down. The last thing I remembered was Jade crying, saying I was dying. But here I was very much alive. My eyes filled with tears again and they continued to stream down the sides of my face.

I tried to sit up, but a sharp pain shot through my chest, causing me fall flat back onto the bed. Closing my eyes, I sighed. I then attempted to roll over on my side, but it felt like a ton of bricks were sitting on me. The pain increased. I almost wanted to scream out in agony, but instead, I bit down hard on my bottom lip. Hearing the door open made me sigh in relief.

COVERED IN YOUR LOVE 2
by *Nique Luarks*

"Jaime?" Nas' voice made me toughen up. I couldn't let him see me cry. I'm sure I looked pathetic enough.

"Yes," I said in a raspy voice before licking my lips.

"I'm 'bout to go get the doc, a'ight?" He came to the side of the bed, rubbing my arm.

I nodded my response and closed my eyes again.

***

I didn't recall falling back to sleep, but when I came to, Duke was staring me right in the face. His fluffy cheeks rose slowly into a cute little smile as he put his face damn near on mine.

"Hi, Mama." He grabbed both sides of my face and kissed my cheek.

"Hey, my bean." I mumbled and then cleared my throat.

"You up now, Mama?" I saw the sadness in my baby's pretty eyes as he let me go.

"She better be." Nas came to the side of the bed, picking up a hospital cup. He fumbled with the bending straw for a second before he put it to my lips.

That first cool sip of ice water was refreshing. Nas held the straw in place as I downed a little more. After quenching my thirst, I licked my lips and placed my eyes back on Duke. He looked like he had a fresh lining and cut. The white T-shirt he had on was crisp, and I didn't recognize the black and white Nike windbreaker he was sporting.

"How long have I been here?" My gaze shifted to Nas.

"Two and a half weeks." He grabbed the remote to call a nurse. "You woke up this morning and passed right back out."

I nodded as Duke lay down next to me. "Mama, you like my new shoes?" he asked, raising his right leg to show me the black Timbs on his tiny feet.

I rested my chin on the top of his head, nodding slowly. "Those are flyy, Bean." I closed my eyes.

"You feeling tired again?" Nas asked, caressing my cheek.

"A little." I wanted to cry. But I needed to be alone to do that.

"What's the matter?" Nas asked me the same time the door flew open.

"Ms. Taylor..." I could hear the smile in her voice. "I'm glad you're awake. How are you feeling?" A middle-aged, black woman holding a clipboard asked.

"Uncomfortable." I admitted. "Can I go home?" I asked her, but looked to Nas like he could give me my answer.

She chuckled. "Not just yet. I want to keep you for a couple of days. Do you remember what happened?"

"I was shot." I looked back up at the ceiling. "Somebody shot me."

Jaime, you better not let them see you cry.

I swallowed, and even that hurt.

"You were shot twice, actually." She flipped through her clipboard. "Once in the hip and once in the chest." She fixed the glasses on her round face.

I closed my eyes.

"We almost lost you." Placing the clipboard to her side, she looked me over slowly. "I can have the nurse increase your pain medication dosage if you get too uncomfortable, okay?"

I shook my head no. "I don't wanna be drowsy." Hell, I'd already missed out on two weeks. *Two weeks.* My heart dropped to the pit of my stomach. Thank God my eyes were closed, because if they'd been open, Nas and the doctor would've seen the tears I was trying so hard to hide.

Dr. Moore rubbed my shoulder. "I'll have the nurse come and check on you in a little while."

I nodded, and she made her exit.

"You hungry?" Nas asked, looking down at his phone.

"No." Eating was the last thing on my mind. I wanted to go home. I wanted to go to my room, close the door, lay across my bed in the dark, and cry.

He sat down in the chair closest to the bed. He nodded, putting his phone to his ear.

"Ouch!" I winced when Duke accidentally kneed me in my stomach. "Be careful, baby."

He nodded, but then he pressed down on my chest to sit himself up.

"Duke...." I was hit by a quick pain near my left breast.

"Duke, my guy, you gotta be careful." Nas stood up and helped him out of the bed. "We gotta nurse ya mama back to health. She won't get better if you beat her up." He chuckled, putting him down.

"I'm sorry, Mama." He went for the iPad sitting on a chair.

"I texted your sister and shit and told her you was up, but she ain't hit me back." He informed me, grabbing the water again. After gently fixing the pillows behind my head, he handed me the cup. "Can you hold it?"

"Yeah." Taking it from him, I placed the straw to my lips and took a long sip. I'd never known water to be so damn good.

"When the nurse come in, we gon' ask what you can eat." He took his seat again.

"I failed my class." I shook my head. "I know I did."

He chuckled.

Huh. I pouted

"Nas, I'm hungry." Duke's small voice made me look at him.

Nas looked over at Duke. "We bout to head out and let ya moms have some alone time."

"I want some nuggets," Duke's little rude butt ordered, looking down at the iPad, playing some game that was making a lot of noise.

Nas shook his head at him.

"Why isn't Duke with Jade?" I asked the million-dollar question I'd been dying to know the answer to since I'd opened my eyes.

"He's been with Jade every Tuesday and Thursday. She claimed she needed him gone for a couple of hours. Crazy broad even tried to push *her* kids on me." He ran his hand across the top of his shiny waves, shaking his head. "That bitch is a train wreck."

"Okay, now." I shot him a look. I wasn't for anybody disrespecting my sisters, right or wrong. I was going to have to have a long talk with Jade Taylor. Why would she think it was okay to pass my son off to a complete stranger? Where was Troy?

He stared back at me unfazed. "I usually drop him back off around nine. When I get him, we hit up a fast food joint and come here." He leaned back into his seat. "Oh, we went to the mall last Thursday and got haircuts today." He looked down at his ringing phone.

What the hell? I frowned.

"Yo." Licking his lips, he answered his phone with his eyes on me. "I told you if it wasn't an emergency don't hit me." His faced contorted into a mug.

Taking another sip of my water, I brought my eyes back to Duke.

"'Cause I'm with my woman, nigga."

Hearing *that* word made my eyes dart right back in his direction. Since when was I his *woman*?

His eyes bore into mine, still unfazed.

"I'ma get with you later, Tito." He hung up with an attitude. "What y'all tryna watch?" He picked the remote up and turned the TV on the same time the nurse entered.

13

After she checked my vitals, scheduled me a shower, and told me I could eat anything I wanted, but keep it light, she was on her way. Adjusting the bed, I tried to get comfortable.

"You need help?" Nas asked, already coming to my assistance.

Once I was settled, thanks to him, he handed me the remote control. Deciding on an episode of *Family Guy*, I rested back into the pillows. Duke's iPad had his undivided attention and Nas was lost in his phone. Twenty minutes later, I was yawning and my eyelids started feeling heavy. The door opened again and a nurse stepped into the room.

"Hey, Jaime. My name is Macy. I'll be helping you with a bath today." She smiled and then looked over at Duke when he ran up on the side of the bed. "Awww, he's so cute. Hi, little man," she gushed.

"I'm not little." Duke watched her intently as she helped me sit up on the side of the bed.

"I'm sorry, big guy." She chuckled.

"My name is Duke."

I shook my head.

"We 'bout to be out." Nas stood up. "Duke, grab your iPad."

14

I didn't know how I felt about him telling my son what to do. Duke, however, did what he was told, tucking his iPad underneath his small arm.

"I'll bring you something to eat later." He started for the door. "Duke, my guy, kiss ya moms bye."

"Bye, Mama," he pouted coming to my side.

"Bye, Bean." I leaned over as far as my body would allow me as he stood on his tippy toes to give me a kiss.

"Nas, can you have Jade call me when you drop him off?" I had a mouthful to say to her irresponsible ass.

"Yeah." He nodded, holding the door open for Duke. "Your phone is in the drawer."

"Okay. I love you, Bean." I started feeling emotional. I didn't want him to go, but I needed to be alone.

"I love you too, Mama."

"He's straight." Nas assured me. "We bout to hit up McDonalds. Then I'm dropping him off. I'ma call you as soon as we pull up to your sister's spot."

I nodded as they left me. The moment the door shut, even though Macy was helping me off the bed, I felt alone. But, hey, at least I was alive.

by *Nique Luarks*

Quan

After Ry left I stood in the street for a second, letting all the shit that had transpired register—Brianna saying she was having my baby, Ryan popping up, and Ry *crying*. Seeing her in tears made it hard to breath for some reason. After I heard her fuckin' another nigga, you I would think I wouldn't give two fucks about her punk-ass tears, but I did a whole lot.

That was damn near three weeks ago, though. Three *long* weeks ago. Shit in my life was chaotic as fuck. I was barely getting any sleep and a nigga couldn't even eat. I didn't know what the fuck was wrong with me.

I'd just left Brianna's doctor's appointment and even seeing my baby on the screen hadn't changed my mood. In all honesty, I'd never thought I would ever have a baby with nobody but Ry. But here I was about to have a baby with her arch enemy. Yeah, shit was all fucked up. Pulling up on the side of Nas' Challenger, I put my whip in park and stepped out.

"What up?" He rolled down his window and we slapped fives.

"I can't call it." He handed me the blunt he was hitting.

I noticed Duke was sitting in the passenger's seat, fuckin' around on an iPhone. "What's up, lil' homie?" I took a pull.

"What's up?" His lil' bad ass kept looking down at the phone.

It was mad crazy seeing Nas play step daddy to a kid. From what he had told me about Jaime, she wasn't even fuckin' wit' him like that. But here the nigga was baby-sitting and cashing out at the mall on him and shit.

"Jaime good?" I handed him the spiff back.

"Yeah, she straight." He nodded. "Any word on who shot that block up?" He looked at his rearview mirror.

"Heard it was some niggas from the Bronx, Tae and them. They had some beef over there, and Jaime just happened to be outside." I shrugged nonchalantly. There were drive-bys in the hood every day. It was unfortunate his shorty got caught in the crossfire, but he was gon' have to charge that to the game.

Again, he nodded.

"What you got up, though?" I asked, looking up the street.

"Shit, drop my guy off and go post up." He hung out the window slightly to give me pound.

"A'ight, I'ma probably slide through later."

He sat back in his seat.

17

"A'ight lil', Duke. Stay up, homie." I chuckled at him, holding a stack of money in his small hands.

Once they drove away, I headed up the stairs and into the trap. I needed to let go of Ryan. Shit with us hadn't worked out, so I had no other option but to move on. I had a shorty coming, and I knew there was no coming back from that. I wished the best for her as I opened the door and stepped into the spot.

Chapter Three

Ice Melts

Jaime

"Be careful." Jade helped me into my bed.

My entire body was sore, but I was happy to finally be home. "I'm not fragile, Jay." I shook my head at her. Jade had picked me up from the hospital an hour ago and she'd been acting like I was precious cargo the whole time. It was sweet of her to be so caring, but I also knew she was trying to make up for dumping Duke off on Nas.

"So, you still need to take it easy." She rolled her eyes as I lay on my side.

"Before you go can you bring me a bottle of water?" I pouted playfully.

"Meme, I love you and all, but we were just downstairs. Why didn't you say something before we got all the way up here?" she complained. "Now, I gotta go downstairs and come all the way back up." She frowned before stepping away from my bed.

"Love you, sissy." I chuckled, fluffing my pillow out.

"Whatever," she mumbled, walking out of the room.

19

COVERED IN YOUR LOVE 2
by *Nique Luarks*

Ten minutes later and just when I was about to call out for Jade, I heard what sounded like Nas' voice. I couldn't make out what he was saying, but from the muffled sound of his deep baritone, I knew he was at the bottom of the staircase. I rose up slowly, frowning and irritated. He had no reason to be here.

Don't get me wrong, Nas was cool and all, but I just wanted a couple of days…hell, *hours* to myself. Between Jaylen calling me every twenty minutes, Jade smothering me, and Troy having Duke until Sunday, my mental state was warped. The only good thing was I no longer felt the need to cry. Instead, I wanted to relax, turn on to the *Lifetime Movie Network* and unwind alone.

I rolled my eyes.

I could still hear Nas' voice when Jade entered my room carrying a bag of popcorn and water.

"Is he your man now? 'Cause the nigga's acting like y'all a couple." She smacked her lips and sat down on the corner of my bed.

"What is he doing?" I reached for the popcorn.

"He's talking on the phone and being rude as hell." She squinted her eyes. "You want me to tell him to leave?"

No she didn't.

Not only had she overstayed her welcome, but she had the nerve to act like she couldn't stand Nas *after* she asked him to babysit her kids.

"No, I'll handle him."

Nas entered my room and Jadee stood up with an attitude. "Meme, I'm about to go. Tell Jaylen to call me." She smacked her lips as she passed by Nasir.

"The fuck you lookin' at me like that for?" His eyebrows furrowed into a mean scowl.

"I'm not even bout to start with you today," she said before making her exit.

After putting the bag of popcorn on my nightstand, I reached for my remote. "Why are you here?" I wasn't trying to be rude, but, I wanted… no, I *needed* a little solitude.

I watched as he kicked his Jordans off and swaggered to my bed. "Where's Duke?" He eyed me, taking a seat by my feet.

"He's with his father." I sighed. "Why are you here? I wanna be alone."

"How long he gon' be gone?" He ignored me and reached for the remote.

"Nas, come on." I frowned. "I need a couple hours to myself." I stared at his profile as he surfed channels.

"For what?"

Is he for real right now?

"For one, because I said want to be alone. I don't have to have a reason for me to want you to leave. This is my house. If I told you that you needed to get the fuck out, you would have no other choice but to go."

He chuckled lightly and I continued.

"Now, I'm trying to be nice. Can you go?" Sitting up a little, I glared at him.

"Yo, Jaime, you lucky I don't hit women." Licking his lips, he looked over at me slowly. The dark look in his eyes made me look down at my lap. "A nigga's trying to look out for your ungrateful ass, but you trying to put me out." He shook his head and tossed the remote. "This shit dead." Standing up, he fixed his jeans. "I'm out."

My voice was stuck in my throat. What did he mean by *this is dead*? Did he mean like with us? Were we dead? Was he done with me?

"You fine, but I ain't no hoe-ass nigga, Ma." He slipped his feet back into his shoes one by one. "Disrespect ain't negotiable wit me." Tucking his gun back in his jeans, he stared at me. "I ain't no cornball-ass nigga."

For the first time since I'd known Nas, he looked like a threat. The deep creases in his forehead, the furrow of his eyebrows, and the evil look in his eyes—his whole demeanor.

Swallowing, I exhaled slowly. I'd never been intimidated by *anyone*. Never been too scared to say the wrong thing. Never wanted to crawl under a rock and hide. Never wanted to disappear, but the fury and rage I saw in his eyes was unnerving.

"I didn't me—"

"Nah, we good. Stay up, shorty." After hitting me with a quick reverse nod, he left my room.

Ryan

I was cleaning up my area when the instructor came and stood near me. "Hey Ryan, everything okay?" she asked, smiling.

I nodded.

"You sure? I see you walking around looking down an—"

"No disrespect, Zora," I cut her off. "Is my attitude affecting my work?" I stopped what I was doing to look at her.

"Uh...no. I'm just saying." She cleared her throat. "If there's anything I can help you with, I would be more than happy to lend a hand."

No, it sounds like you're being nosey.

I continued to stare at her. Regardless of my *mood*, I came to class every day on time. I was surpassing most of the woman in the class, and my tuition was paid off. Anything that pertained to my life outside of this building was none of her business. Crossing my arms over my chest, I looked her up and down.

"If you need anything before you go..." She looked away awkwardly. "I'll be in my office." Turning on her heels, she rushed away.

I watched her disappear into her office before going back to putting my belongings up. The Louboutin's on my feet clicked against the hard floor as I made sure everything was in place. I started a mental checklist as I went for my leather jacket on the back of the chair. Once my jacket was on I had adjusted it, and I pulled my twenty-four-inch ponytail out of the back. Cutting the lights to my station off, I grabbed my keys, purse, and phone and headed out of the door.

I made it outside to my matte black 2017 Ford Mustang just as it started sprinkling. Unlocking the door, I got in and tossed my purse onto the passenger's seat. Hitting the start button, I went to plug my phone into the charger as Remy Ma bumped loudly from the speakers. Pulling out of the parking lot, I removed a freshly rolled blunt from the console and lit it as I came up on a red light.

Turning the radio up, I took a hit. Exhaling from my nostrils, I pulled off, bobbing my head to the music. Glancing at the clock on the dashboard, I was happy to see I was making good timing. I'd told Lenora I would help her go through her Christmas decorations so she could start putting them up the day after Thanksgiving. It was mad crazy how I went from not trusting her to being her own personal little holiday helper.

I chuckled.

COVERED IN YOUR LOVE 2
by *Nique Luarks*

The rain picked up as I jumped on the highway. An incoming call from Blaze flashed across the screen of my iPhone as I put the blunt out. I hadn't spoken to Blaze since I'd returned from New York. It was nothing against her; I just didn't want to deal with anything or anybody who had ties to DaQuan. Turning the radio down, I grabbed for my phone and answered against my better judgment.

"Well, well, well." I grinned. "If ain't Kai Money's wife."

She giggled. "Hey, Ry."

"Hey, lady. What's up?" I asked, switching lanes.

"Nothing really. I was calling to check on you. You left in a hurry, so I figured I'd give you space and time before I called to bother you."

I respected that.

"Is everything okay on your end?"

"Yeah, everything's straight. I started cosmetology school last week." I pushed down quickly on my brakes. "Watch the fuckin' road!" I yelled at a white, box Chevy as it zoomed past me and down the highway.

Non-driving muthafucka. I rolled my eyes.

"Whaaat?" Blaze sang in my ear. "Congratulations, Ry. You are cold with makeup,." she complimented me.

by *Nique Luarks*

"Thanks. You are too." It made sense, though. Blaze could paint and draw her ass off. I guess being able to hook her makeup up came naturally.

"Well, I'm happy for you. Just make sure you remember the little people when you start working on celebrities," she joked, making me laugh.

"Forget about the family? Girl, please." I shook my head.

"So, everything's good, right?" She sounded concerned. "You don't need anything?"

"Nah, I'm straight." And I was. I was content. I was working on *me*.

"Okay, well, I have to go. I'll catch up with you later." And with that she hung up.

Twenty minutes later after I'd stopped at the gas station, I pulled into Kenya's driveway. Making sure I had all of my shit, I got out. Shutting the car door with my hips, I started towards the house. The loud bass of what I knew to be a crazy stereo system could be hard coming down the block. I stopped in my tracks to watch a white, box Chevy come to a crazy stop in front of Lenora's house.

I should've known. I rolled my eyes at Sy as he got out being loud as hell, talking to the people in his ride.

Continuing my route into the house, I reached the door when I heard him call out to me. "You can't speak?"

"I don't talk to strangers," I said loud enough from him to hear, throwing the deuces over my shoulder as I stepped onto the porch.

***

It took me fifteen minutes to throw on some black tights, a white V-neck, slip my feet into my red Uggs, and put on my army fatigue Parka. Locking up the house, I made my way across the street. I was glad when I didn't see Sy's car. As I made my way up her porch stairs I could hear Con Funk Shun's "Loves Train" bumping from inside. I smiled.

After tapping lightly on the screen door and ringing the door bell, I waited patiently for her to come to the door while bobbing my head to the music. I could smell the chicken she was frying and my stomach rumbled, reminding I hadn't eaten all day.

"Hey, Ryan." Lenora's face appeared not too long after, smiling of course. Unlocking the screen door, she pushed the door open for me, dancing.

COVERED IN YOUR LOVE 2
by *Nique Luarks*

I laughed as I shut the door behind me. Lenora had some rhythm to her. I shook my head as she held her arms out to take my hands.

"Come on and two step wit' me." She grinned moving coolly.

I chuckled.

"If by chance you let me just hold yaaaa," she sang, taking my right hand into hers. "Can you two step?"

I shook my head no. I could Jamaican wind all day. When Quan and I turned twenty-one we were always at my one of my favorite Jamaican spots. Those dates stopped after a while, though. I guess he got too comfortable. I missed those times.

"Every woman should know how to two step." Lenora snapped me from my thoughts as she led me into her living room. "Keep up now," she said, never missing a beat.

I was genuinely entertained as she showed me the steps even when I missed the move trying to be cute. We laughed when she dropped it down low and then had the nerve to pick it up slow. We danced as we sang and grooved to the music. I sang my part and she sang hers in sync, snapping her fingers to the beat with her cool ass. Grabbing my arm, she spun me around, making me laugh harder.

The song got low as it came to an end and she let me go. Sashaying away, she continued to hum under her breath. Stopping at the entrance to the dining room, she faced me. "Hey, Ry." A serious expression graced her face.

"Yeah?" I was now in a vibrant mood.

"If it's meant to be, it will be, but if you want it, go get it."

Chapter Four

By Any Means

Quan

Pulling the black ski mask over my face, I made sure my gloves were secure before I cocked my glock. Nas passed me the blunt and turned the radio down. Even after I told the nigga his shorty wasn't a target in the drive-by, them niggas did, he wasn't trying to hear it. That's why we were currently sitting in front of Tae's mama's house. Raising my mask over my mouth, I took a long pull and then sat the joint in the ashtray.

Getting out of his whip, we made our way up the walkway. He led the way holding a chop. I shook my head at how hot he was not wearing a mask. Once we got on the raggedy porch and to the door, Nas blew the lock off. Almost immediately, I heard screams and what sounded like a stampede of people running throughout the house.

"Oh my God!" a shorty yelled, running towards the back of house.

Nas aimed his chop at her, but quickly put it on a cat that was trying to run down the basement steps. One bullet hit dude in the back and the second one went right through his dome, sending him flying down the basement stairs head first. Shorty almost made it out the back door, but he swiftly turned his banger on her and shot her in the leg. She fell down hard onto the floor, screaming and crying at the top of her fuckin' lungs. Turning on his heels, Nas calmly stalked past me.

This nigga, son.

I chuckled, high as fuck. The fact that he was in his feelings over this Jaime chick was mad wild. I followed him up the stairs where all the noise seemed to be coming from as a little girl suddenly stood at the top, crying. She couldn't have been no older than six. Soon after, a figure appeared right behind her, and I let off one shot, hitting him between the eyes.

"Aaaaaagh!" she yelled, cowering as Nas rushed up the steps.

We stepped past dude's body and separated down the hallway. I heard Nas' gun go off a few times just as a closet door flew open and a chick jumped out letting off a shot that grazed my arm. Smashing her over the head with the handle of my glock, she hit the floor unconscious. Rushing down the other side of the hallway, I could hear Nas talking as I passed two bodies

"Nas, come on, blood. Why are you doing this, B?"

COVERED IN YOUR LOVE 2
by *Nique Luarks*

Entering a bedroom, I watched as Nas stood over Tae. One of his eyes was swollen shut, his nose looked like it was broken, and blood was dripping out of his mouth and covering his white shirt.

I aimed my gun at him the same time Nas did and we both emptied our clips into his body. Running out of the room, we rushed down the hallway past the little girl who was crying softly, down the stairs. Then we ran right out the front door. Jumping in Nas' whip, we peeled off down the street and away from the crime scene. Yanking my ski mask off, I opened the glove compartment and put it and my burner inside. Leaning back into my seat, I reached down in the side of the door for my phone. I frowned when I saw I had twenty-six missed calls from Brianna. Thinking something was wrong with my baby, I called her back. She answered with an attitude.

"What do you want?"

"The fuck you mean? Why you been blowing my phone up Bre?" Nas handed me the blunt.

"What bitch are you with? Why haven't you been answering the phone?" she snapped.

Blowing a cloud of smoke from my nostrils, I shook my head. "Yo, Bre, don't call my phone trippin'."

"I haven't talked to you all day." Her voice softened.

"I saw you earlier." I passed the smoke back to Nas.

"That was at like eleven this morning, though."

"I told you I had some shit to handle."

"I miss you."

And?

When I was with Ry, I used to leave in the middle of the night sometimes. Wouldn't come back till the next day if shit got too hectic, and she'd call me twice. The first time to tell me she loved me and the second to remind me to eat. She never blew my phone up and she never tripped with me about being out all day. She knew I was out trying to secure the bag and our future.

"Bre, I told you I would get wit' you later," I reminded her forgetful ass.

"Well, what time will you be back? Why won't you just move all your clothes over here?" she whined.

Taking the L back from Nas, I inhaled deeply.

"Are you are ignoring me?" Brianna continued to bitch. "I'm pregnant and you got me up in the middle of the night worried about your ass."

Exhaling, I cleared my throat. "Then go to sleep."

"See? Be here before the morning, DaQuan."

"I'll see you when I see you, Brianna."

"For real, Quan? I—"

I ended the call, shaking my head. I used to never get headaches, but since finding out about Brianna's pregnancy, a nigga stayed with a migraine.

"You straight?" Nas asked, bending a corner.

"Yeah. Bre's ass is annoying as fuck."

He chuckled, coming up on a stop sign. "I told you when you first started fuckin' wit that bird to leave her hoe ass alone. Now, you stuck wit' her for life."

"Eighteen years," I mumbled, scrolling through my photos.

"That's life, B." He shook his head, turning up the music.

"Damn near."

I stared down at the last picture I'd taken of Ryan. I'd come in late and she was lying knocked out, butt-ass naked across the bed. I could tell she'd fallen asleep waiting on me because of the candles burning low throughout our bedroom. And her red heels were still on. I took the picture right before I woke her up and made it up to her all night for spoiling her surprise.

Closing out of the picture, I took another pull from the spliff and passed it back. Staring out of my window, I wondered what Ry was doing. She was probably doing her makeup, painting her toes or watching a scary movie. I chuckled lightly thinking about how she loved watching that weird shit even though she was scared of the dark. Facing forward, I licked my lips and ran my hand across my waves. Whatever she was doing, I hoped she knew I missed her lil' gangster ass a whole bunch.

Nas

I don't respect niggas who do drive-bys. That's punk shit. Real gunners, real niggas, who wanted to settle *real* beef didn't hang out of windows shooting up blocks harming innocent women and children. Even though I wasn't fuckin' with Jaime like that, them niggas still needed to be dealt with. She could've died or worse. What if I would've been carrying Duke outside and he'd been hit? Jaime would've hurt forever over that.

Coming to a stop in front of Tami's crib, I put my whip in park and hopped out irritated. Jaime had me fucked up. When she was talkin' all that rah-rah shit, I almost yoked her little ass up and strangled her. That's why I had to get the fuck out of there. I'd never let a bitch talk to me like that. *Nobody* talk to me like that.

I let myself into Tami's spot and the smell of a cooked meal hit my nostrils, calming me down a little.

"Nas?" She came around the corner in nothing but a purple, lace bra and panty set. Her long, curly hair was all over the place.

"What up?" I asked, making my way to the living room. I tossed my keys onto the end table as she made her entrance.

"Everything good?" Taking a seat next to me, she looked over me innocently. "Did somebody—"

"Nah, ain't nobody get smoked."

She blew out a sigh of relief. "You hungry?"

"Yeah, hook me up." I reached for the remote and she stood up.

Fifteen minutes later, I was watching ESPN, smashing the cheesy rice, BBQ chicken, corn, and Hawaiian rolls Tami had put on my plate. Trying to keep up with the highlights for the day's game, Jaime's lil' mean ass crossed my mind.

Bipolar ass.

"You look like you got a lot on your mind." She put her plate down.

"Nah..." I quickly brushed off her attempt to read me.

"Okay, well, have you talked to Nikki?" she asked, referring to my crazy, irresponsible, reckless-ass older sister.

"Nah?" I shook my head. "Why?" I asked, still looking at the TV.

"She was in her feelings about Kai. Ever since he and that bitch Bla—"

by *Nique Luarks*

"Yo..." I cut her off mid-sentence. Blaze was my family too. "Call my sis another bitch." Sitting my plate down, I reached for my water.

"Are you serious?"

"Dead ass."

"Nikki is you blood sister. She knew Kai first and she held him down for years. And he goes and shits on her for a bitch he done known for like only two weeks." She rolled her eyes and reached for her plate.

Before she could grab it, I snatched her by her arm and yanked her stupid ass towards me. "What the fuck did I just say?" I glared at her.

"But—"

"Ain't no fuckin' buts. That ain;t got shit to do wit' me or you. Mind your fuckin' business," I demanded, pushing her away roughly.

Snatching up her plate, she stormed out of the room.

Sighing, I leaned back into my seat. I closed my eyes and silently prayed Tami wouldn't make me put my hands on her by the end of the night. I wasn't into whooping on bitches, but all that mouthy shit these hoes had been on lately was getting out of control. It was like I had to press a hard line to make a point

39

nowadays. I usually only had to give Tami a look and she knew to shut the fuck up.

But then there was lil' mean-ass Jaime. I opened my eyes when I felt Tami's presence and she dropped down in front of me. Taking my burner off my hip, I sat it down on the couch next to me. She unbuckled my pants and undid my button. Helping her, I pulled my dick out of the top of my briefs.

It was mad wild how even though I was looking down at Tami, I wished it was Jaime. Don't get me wrong, Tami was dope as fuck. She had pretty skin, nice body, no kids, and she was all about her paper. She was just a messy-ass hood rat that loved running the streets and setting niggas up. Her and Nikki.

I watched as she swallowed my dick and my mind went back to Jaime Taylor. The way she moaned when she was cumming. Them pretty eyes. Her smell. That smile.

Shit.

I closed my eyes.

"Mmmm…" Tami moaned.

Planting my palm on the back of her head, I guided her down further with one thing on my mind—Jaime Taylor. How soft her lips were. The sexy switch in her walk. That damn smile.

Fuck.

COVERED IN YOUR LOVE 2
by *Nique Luarks*

Tami was putting in some serious work, but my mental was on *her*, Jaime fuckin' Taylor. How tight her pussy was. How hard she came. The way she called out my name. That goddamn smile.

"Fuck..." A deep groan escaped my lips and that was all she wrote.

Tami took every drop of my nut down, making sure she got it all. Standing up quickly, she made room for me to stand up and fix my clothes. Once I was straight, I put my burner back on my waist and grabbed my phone and keys.

"You leaving already?" she pouted. "I wanted some dick."

"I got you next time, shorty." I made my way back to the front door.

"So, I'll see you later on today?" she pressed as I went to open the door.

"Is that what I said?" I stopped moving to look down at her.

Instead of answering me, she frowned.

"I'ma get wit' you later. Lock the door."

Chapter Five

I fumbled your heart

Ryan

Three days before Christmas…

Here I was *again*. Another year had flown by since she'd been gone. Going into a squatting position, I took the lilies in my hand and placed them against my grandmother's headstone. The cold December wind brushed across my face, making my eyes water just a little.

"I miss you," I whispered, staring at the picture of her on her headstone. "So much."

I hadn't been to my grandmother's gravesite since my birthday in April for good reasons. Even though she'd been gone five years now, I was still hurting from her absence.

"Grammy, I'm all alone. Why did you leave me here by myself?" I choked up. "You were all I had." I hung my head.

Running my hand across her picture, it was then that I noticed another set of lilies resting to the right of her headstone. Picking them, I could see they weren't fresh, but they weren't out-dated either. Sitting them back down, I stared at her headstone as tears welled in my eyes. Whenever I was sad, she'd always tell me to pray. But I hadn't talked to God in so long that I didn't even know what to say or how to even start.

This shit wasn't fair. My life wasn't fair. Since birth, I'd been dealt a shitty hand and I was tired. Physically, I was strong, but emotionally, I'd been hanging on by a single thread. But Quan had cut that in half a long time ago.

I could hear footsteps behind me thanks to the frozen ground being frozen over. Pulling my glock from the small of my back, I kept my eyes trained on my grammy. I quickly remembered it was Christmas time and a lot of people came out here to pay respect, so I needed to chill. But then.a familiar scent hit my nostrils. I didn't look up at him, though; not even when he placed over two dozen fresh lilies on her grave.

"I didn't think you were coming." His deep voice opened the flood gates to the all the pain I'd buried right along with my grandmother.

"Why are you here?" I still didn't look at him. I couldn't, because if I did, I'd probably feel obligated to shoot him.

"When have I ever missed a visit?" he asked in a condescending tone.

COVERED IN YOUR LOVE 2
by *Nique Luarks*

I finally glanced up at him. "You didn't have to come." I tried to ignore how good he looked. how sexy he was, and how fast my heart was beating in my chest.

"Yeah, I did." He shrugged nonchalantly, adjusting the red Jordan skull cap on his head.

"Well, thanks, but you can go now," I snapped, giving my attention back to my grandmother.

He didn't leave. Instead, he came down into a jail pose next to me. "Did you pray yet?"

"No." And I didn't plan to.

"Bow your head."

What? No. I shook my head. For what? Nah, I didn't want to pray. I wanted to finish out the rest of this visit, go back to my hotel, and drink my misery away. I'd pray another day.

"Yo, Ry, I know shit wit' us is fucked up." He paused. "And it's my fault."

Well, you don't say? I rolled my eyes.

"And regardless of what you might think, I love the fuck outta you, Ma." He sighed.

"DaQuan, don't." I stood up. I couldn't even visit my favorite lady in peace. He followed suit as I took one last look at her headstone, prepared to walk away.

44

"Man, Ry..." He said, grabbing me by my forearm. He made me face him. "Bow your fuckin' head, yo."

I kindly snatched away from him. "Why do you care?" He was starting to piss me off.

"Cause it's what she would've wanted. I get that you mad at me, but quit acting like a fuckin' brat."

I hated him. I hated even more that he was right. Grammy had made me promise on her death bed to always pray when things got too rough and to come see her no matter how hard it was. I just didn't want to pray with *him*. I'm sure my grandmother was turning over in her grave, disappointed in the both of us.

Looking off into the distance, I sighed in defeat and I bowed my head.

***

We walked back to the road in silence until Quan's phone went off. Removing his iPhone from the pocket of his black puffer coat, he answered just as we made it to my rental.

"Yo..."

Hitting the unlock button on the key fob, I opened the driver's door.

"Yeah, I'm wit' her right now. Hold on." He came to my side trying to hand me his phone.

I looked down at it like he had shit all over his hand.

"Nas wanna rap wit' you."

Taking his phone from him, I put it on speaker. "What, Nas?"

He chuckled. "Don't *what* me, nigga. What's good, sis? I ain't talked to your crazy ass in a while. You straight?"

"Everything's cool on my end." Even though Nas owed all his loyalty to Quan, he was still on my shit list. I'd known Nas just as long as I'd known DaQuan. I wasn't fuckin' with him right now, but he would always be family.

"You should come out tonight. Blaze is throwing a Christmas party. Come kick it wit' yo big bro, man. I know you mad at me."

I shook my head as if he could see me. "Nah, I'll pass."

He sucked his teeth. "A'ight. Well, check it. Stay up, sis. I'ma get wit' you later."

"One." I handed Quan his phone back.

"Where you staying? Is it far?" He looked up as it started snowing. "You know you can't drive." He smiled, displaying the dimple in his left cheek and his pretty, perfect Colgate smile.

COVERED IN YOUR LOVE 2
by *Nique Luarks*

The wind picked up. "I'm like twenty minutes away. And have you forgotten who used to be the getaway driver?" I got in the car.

"Yo, Ry..." He stopped me from shutting the door and licked his lips.

Fine ass… Again, I rolled my eyes.

"Come to Madame X's wit' ya boy."

The look on my face must have been a dead giveaway for *fuck no*, because he smiled again.

"One drink. Where's your holiday spirit?"

"It died. Three days before Christmas to be exact." The minute they dropped my grammy's casket into the earth.

His face went soft. "Well, either you come have a drink wit' me or I'ma follow you to your room and sing Christmas carols outside your door all night."

I frowned. Quan was always trying to sing to me, knowing damn well he couldn't hold a tune.

"You are annoying as fuck." I started the car.

He grinned. "I'm following you."

Quan

I couldn't wipe the stupid grin I knew was plastered on my face as I followed Ryan. A nigga was too geeked that she gave in. I hadn't been in her presence in a while, so a nigga was really feeling like a big-ass kid on Christmas morning. I'd come to her grandmother's gravesite to lay out her favorite flowers and swap out the old ones. I knew Ry would probably come out, but God was lookin' out making sure we crossed paths.

Pulling into the parking lot of Madame X's, I maneuvered around until I found a parking spot. Surprisingly, we both found one quick and close to the door. Hopping out of my whip, I put my burner on my waist and bent down to fix the shoe strings on my red Jordan 11's.

"Can you hurry up?" Ryan's sexy-ass voice made my dick brick up in the dead of winter.

"I'm coming rude ass." I rose up to look down on her pretty face. "Did you eat anything?" We made our way towards the entrance.

"I'm not hungry." She mumbled, looking down at her phone.

"Yo, Ry, you know I don't like you drinking on an empty stomach."

"Well, luckily for you, I'm not your responsibility no more," she hissed with her smart-ass mouth, still looking at that damn phone.

Hitting the bouncer with a reverse nod, I put my hand on the small of Ry's back as she led the way inside. The loud reggae music blaring from the speakers had muthafuckas on the dance floor practically fuckin'. Following Ry to a vacant booth, she took a seat and I took one right next to her. Resting my right arm behind her head, I leaned in close to her and kissed the back of her ear where the words "My Ry" were tatted.

She quickly moved her head away from me with a frown on her face. "You need to back the fuck up." She wiped my kiss off.

"So, I can't kiss on you now?" I stared at her.

"I don't know where your lips have been." She stared back at me.

"Hey, Ry! Long time no see, girl! Where the hell you been?"

I kept my eyes on Ry as she pulled hers away from me to look at ole girl.

"Hey, Cameron." She smiled. "Girl, I moved."

"Really? Where to?" Nosy asked.

"Missouri." Ryan's eyes landed back on mine. "Aint nothing here in New York for me. I needed a fresh, new start." She brought her eyes back to Cameron.

"Oh... I see Quan and Nas around all the time and—"

"We'll take two blue muthafuckas and four shots of Patron," I cut in, finally giving her my attention. She was doing too much talking.

"Don't be a rude ass." Ry rolled her eyes, picking up her phone. "I still got your number. girl. I'll text you." She smiled. It had to be a crime to be *that* stunning.

I noticed Ry was rocking her real hair and it was a honey color, stopping at her shoulders. As always her makeup was done to perfection and she smelled good as fuck enhanced by her favorite fragrance, Chanel No. 5. I watched as she removed her coat and fixed her black, off-the-shoulder bodysuit. The shit was revealing and I almost snapped on her fast ass, but I had to remember she wasn't mine no more.

"Why are you staring at me?" She picked her phone up, bobbing her head to the music.

I hadn't even noticed that ole girl had walked away. "It's hard not to." I leaned in, kissing that tattoo again.

"*DaQuan...*" she huffed, wiping my kiss off again. "I don't know what you think this is, but it ain't that, yo," she snapped. "Where the fuck is your baby mama? She needs to come get her nigga." She mugged me.

"Man..."

"Man my ass." Her mugged deepened.

"Two blue muthafuckas. I had Barry make them extra strong." Cameron slid our glasses in front of us. "And four shots of Patron on the house, of course." She placed the shots on the table and skipped off.

Ryan took her first shot to the head before she reached for her drink. I continued to stare at her as she sipped pretty, vibing to the music. Taking both of my shots, I looked around the joint, making sure shit didn't look out of the norm.

"So, how long you here for?" I grabbed my glass up.

"Till Wednesday. I promised Blaze we would go have a spa day and go shopping." She looked over at me.

Stunning.

I licked my lips. My eyes roamed over her frame, noticing she'd lost weight. I frowned.

"You ain't been eating?"

"When I have an appetite." She took a long sip of her drink.

I nodded. "What you been on in Missouri besides the next nigga's dick?"

Son, if looks could kill... I tried not to kiss her little scrunched up nose.

"Quan, don't start shit you know you can't finish. I had sex with him *after* we broke up. It ain't my fault you popped up unannounced and uninvited." She quickly finished off the rest of her drink.

"Thirsty?" I smirked.

"No. I'm bored." She picked up her phone again.

"Still mean, I see."

"Some things never change." She picked up her second shot and tossed it back.

"Yeah, they don't," I said, scooting closer to her to grip the inside of her thigh. It was wild how I could say I couldn't stand her because she fucked ole dude, but here I was unable to keep my hands and mouth off of her. Crazy.

"You're mighty touchy." She tried to remove my hand, but of course, I was stronger than she was, so I didn't budge.

"More shots?" Cameron came from out of nowhere.

"Yeah. Bring us four more," I addressed her, but kept my gaze on Ry's fine ass.

"Be right back." She walked off as Ry tried to pry my hand off of her again.

She gave up. "Can you move?"

"Nah, my hand is cold."

"And?" She frowned.

"The heat from your pussy is keeping it warm."

She blushed. "Quan."

"Ryan?"

"Get your hand off me please and stop putting your lips on me."

I chuckled, knowing I'd struck a nerve. "Yo, you fine as fuck, Keyshia." I grinned, fucking with her.

She tried to hide her smile. "Wish I could say the same about you."

"You can't?" I leaned in closer.

"Nope."

"Lie again," I whispered in her ear before licking her earlobe.

"I swear y'all are so damn cute." Mouthy came back with shots.

"Ugh, girl no. I don't even fuck wit' him like that no more." She reached for her two shots.

"Oh…" Cameron cleared her throat awkwardly.

Ry's drunk ass tossed both of her shots back. Nodding her head up and down, she reached for another shot. "Umhm, got a whole baby on the way with that hoe, Brianna."

"What!?" Cameron gasped in shock. "Ry—"

"Yo, shorty, get away from this table." I looked up at her. "Don't come back over here either." I waved her off and she quickly switched away.

"Don't get mad at her cause you couldn't keep your dick in your pants and it finally caught up to you." She threw a shot back. "Just stupid." Shaking her head, she reached for the fourth shot.

Snatching it out of her hand, I tossed it back.

"You destroyed me, Quan." She looked over at me sadly.

"I know, man." I sighed, sitting the shot glass down. "I fucked up. You the best thing that ever happened to me, Ryan. I ain't never met nobody who'd ride for me as hard as you did. Shit, I probably never will." I ran my hands down my face in frustration. "You should be the one having my baby."

She chuckled. "You are so right about that."

"But like Grammy used to always tell us: God does everything for a reason. Right?" I asked, tucking a piece of her hair behind her ear. "Maybe God knew you were too good for me."

It hurt like a muthafucka to think that, but to say it out loud? A nigga was in his feelings overtime. Ry was going to end up with a nigga that was going to love her better than I did. Damn. Sitting back in my seat, I looked off towards the dance floor.

"I'm sorry, Ryan." Looking back over at her, I felt like I'd just taken a major loss. And in a way I had.

"Aye, that's life, right? You win some and you lose some." She stared at me intently.

"That's what they say." I stared back at my baby.

She nodded.

The beat dropped and Shaggy's "Boombastic" started playing. I chuckled lightly.

"What's so funny?" She bumped me playfully.

"This song, man. When you first heard it, you played this shit out, yo." I groaned, shaking my head. Once Ry heard a song she liked, she played the shit until you wanted to break her phone. That Versace on the Floor joint used to irritate the fuck out of me. But I knew that shit by heart.

She laughed, hitting me. "Whatever. This is *still* the shit." She moved her hips in her seat.

"Oh, you still got it?" I checked her out.

"What kind of question is that?" She grinned, still dancing, eyes low.

"Ah shit." I slid out of the booth. "I thought you might've gone to Missouri and squared up on me," I joked as she scooted out of the booth, smiling.

"Boy, please." She stood up, winding her hips. "I know you heard the way old dude was moaning when I was putting it down." She clasped her hand over her mouth before she burst into a fit of laughter.

I didn't find shit funny. "Man…" I drawled. I was mad all over again. I hadn't even addressed that shit and for good reasons.

"Oh shut up." She pulled me along as she headed for the dance floor, still laughing at my expense.

We made it to the packed dance floor and Ry turned to face me. She looked up at me seductively, moving her body all sexy and shit. Mouthing the words to song, I watched her go into her zone.

Damn, I love you.

Winding her hips, she turned around placing her ass on me. Bending over slightly, she popped to the beat, fuckin' my head up. Grabbing her hips, I pulled her closer to me. Standing up straight, she started grinding on my dick. Laying her head into my chest, she closed her eyes, grinding on me. I took the opportunity to plant a wet kiss on her neck. She quickly turned back around and looked up at me.

It was like time stood still or some shit as she stopped dancing and we stared at one another. Pulling her closer to me, I caressed my thumb across the tattoo behind her ear. Resting my forehead on hers, I closed my eyes, and son, it was like I could literally feel my heart being yanked out of my chest. This could possibly be the last time I'd hold *my Ry* in my arms. I opened my eyes to find her staring back at me.

The sad look in her eyes told me she was thinking the same thing. Gently grabbing both sides of her face, I kissed her soft lips. At first she tried to pull away, but when I slid my right hand across the side of her neck and pulled her closer by the back of her head, she surrendered. If this was going to be the last time, then I was going to make it count.

Chapter Six

Drunk in Love

Ryan

I don't know what came over me. Staring back at Quan, I pushed my body away from him. Taking a deep breath, I then took a step back. Looking down at my feet, I sighed.

Only Quan could make me feel so vulnerable. When I was with him I was reminded it was okay to be soft. It was okay to have feelings and it was okay to be myself, a woman. The beat changed as he gripped my chin and made me look up at him. Leaning in close, his lips brushed across my earlobe making me shudder.

"Let me rap wit' you real fast." His deep baritone rumbled my core.

"About what?" I leaned in closer to him.

"Come found out." He nonchalantly pulled me through the crowd, heading towards the exit.

"My coat..." I looked over my shoulder to our booth.

"I'll buy you another one." He led me out into the cold brisk air.

Following him to his car, he opened the passenger's side for me to get in. After he shut my door, I watched him swagger to the driver's side and hop in. Instantly, butterflies filled my stomach. After he started his ride he gripped the inside of my thigh and gave it a soft squeeze.

***

Fifteen minutes later, and after an awkwardly silent car ride, we were at the Marriot riding the elevator up to the thirteenth floor. We both stood quietly the entire way up. I was lost in my thoughts as he stared at me intently. Even though I was facing forward, I could see him in my peripheral vision. He licked his lips and absentmindedly ran his hand across the top of his head.

Stop staring at me.

I hated how nervous he was making me feel.

"You a'ight?" he finally spoke as the elevator came to a stop and the doors slid open.

"I'm straight." I followed behind him.

"You sure?" he asked over his shoulder as we came up on room 1326.

by *Nique Luarks*

"Umhm..." I mumbled, stepping into the room. Shutting the heavy door behind me, I pressed my back against it and closed my eyes.

What are you doing, Ry? I knew better than this shit.

I opened my eyes again slowly only to find Quan standing right in front of me.

Picking me up, he carried me into the kitchen area and sat me down on the counter. Opening my legs wider so he could come closer, he roughly lifted my shirt over my head. Sucking on my collar bone and neck, he unhooked my bra and released my breasts.

"Ooooh..." I whimpered as his tongue flicked across my nipple. A sharp tingle shot through my pussy as his warm tongue trailed up my chest.

"I love you, baby." He bit down on my bottom lip. "I'm sorry."

Helping him pull his shirt over his head, I attacked his neck. Sucking, licking, and kissing all over the front of his neck where *Ryan* was tatted in big, bold, black cursive writing. In one quick motion he lifted me up slightly and yanked my jeans down. Once they were to my ankles, he yanked them clean off, leaving me only in my heels.

COVERED IN YOUR LOVE 2
by *Nique Luarks*

Unbuckling his belt, he undid the button on his jeans. Pushing me back further onto the sink and spreading my legs, he kissed the inside of my thighs. Planting hickeys inside my thighs, his warm lips latched onto my throbbing clit. I let out a soft whimper as he flicked his tongue across my pearl.

"Mmmm..." he moaned into my love.

"Sssshit." I bit down on my bottom lip. "Mmm... Right there, baby." I started grinding my hips.

My eyes rolled to the back of my head when he started fucking me with his tongue. On the verge of cumming, I grabbed the sides of his head, squeezing my eyes shut. My entire body rocked as I released a much-needed orgasm. My clit immediately became sensitive as he pressed down on it with his tongue. I tried to break from his grasp, but he had a strong hold on me.

"Wait." His tongue slithered all over my kitty, driving me crazy. "Qu-Quan," I muttered, my legs shaking, heart racing, and my mind gone.

When he slid two fingers inside me my eyes popped open the same time wet lips connected with mine.

"Baby..." I whimpered.

by *Nique Luarks*

"I love you, Ry," he whispered into my mouth. "I love you, baby. I'm sorry, man." His thumb attacked my clit as his fingers slammed repeatedly against my G-spot.

"God..." I froze and I'm sure the look on my face was one for a good laugh as I came harder than I had in my entire life.

What the fuck?

My legs shook, but Quan didn't stop hitting my spot even when I started squirting all over his stomach and chest.

"Aaaagh!" I tried to push him back as he pulled his fingers out and rubbed his entire hand across my pussy, making me squirt harder. "Quaaaan...."

I was still in a daze when he picked me up and slid me down the length of his shaft. The shit felt so good. So, so good. Like home. Wrapping my arms around his neck, I stuck my tongue in his mouth.

"I missed you, Mama," he moaned.

Ignoring him, I started fucking him back.

"You ain't miss me?" he groaned.

Hell yeah, I missed him a whole bunch, but I wasn't about to tell him that.

"I can feel you in my stomach." I picked up the pace, throwing my head back.

"Mmm...hol' up, baby." He held onto my hips firmly.

"Uhmmm..." I moved my hips in a circular motion.

"Fuck..." He sighed.

"I'm bout to cum," I said, staring in his eyes. And soon after, a third orgasm ripped through my body, damn near making me pass out.

As I came all over him, I could feel his dick pulsating inside of me; jerking hard.

"I love you," he muttered.

***

I opened my eyes only for my vision to be blurry. Rubbing my eyes, I cleared my throat. I could still feel the effects of the alcohol I'd consumed so fast. Lifting my head, I looked around the dimly-lit room. My eyes than roamed over to the clock on the night stand.

1:23a.m.

"I need to go," I spoke to myself, attempting to get out of the bed. I didn't feel guilty or stupid for what we'd done, but I needed to put some distance between us. I needed to sober up.

"Where you going?" Quan asked, grabbing my forearm.

"Home." I kept my back to him.

COVERED IN YOUR LOVE 2
by *Nique Luarks*

"Nah, you not." Pulling me close, he lifted me up, laying my body on top of his.

"Quan, I'm sore." I tried to wiggle free.

"So." His tongue snaked across my neck as his manhood hardened. "I ain't done wit' you."

I shuttered.

His mouth found mine and our tongues danced around coolly. Grabbing his dick, I led him into my opening. We continued kissing as he filled me up. I swear it should be against the law for dick to be so good. It had to be.

Planting my feet flat on the bed on both sides of him I began riding slowly. Resting my hands on his chest, I went to work. Clinching my pussy muscles around his thickness, I bounced up and down, popping my butt. Besides our moans, all you could hear was the sound of him plunging into my wetness and my ass slapping against his legs. My mouth fell agape when I felt myself cumming.

"Uh..." I tried to keep my momentum up, but Quan leaned forward, wrapped his arms around my waist and latched onto my right nipple, playing with my nipple ring.

"Yeah, cum for Daddy," he urged, thrusting his hips.

"Baby..."

64

"This is what you needed, huh?" his cocky ass asked, going harder.

"*Yesss*!" I screamed, unable to handle the euphoria. "Fuck this pussy." I attempted to throw it back, but he wasn't having it.

"This pussy so good, Ma," he moaned, continuing to slam me down. "Come all over this muthafucka."

And I did. As a matter of fact, he made me cum all night. Morning too.

Chapter Seven

Know the difference

Jaime

"Bean, put your coat back on." I turned in my seat to look at him

"I don't wanna wear a coat." He frowned.

Opening my door, I sighed. It was like Duke's daily mission was to disobey everything I said. Shutting my door, I traveled to his side of the car, opened the door, and helped him out. I then shut his door and helped him put his coat back on.

"You ready to see your dad, Bean?" I asked, fixing his Nike skull cap.

"No. I wanna see *Nas*." He looked up at me.

I frowned. "Nas?" I hadn't seen or talked to him in weeks. Duke wanting to see him instead of his father bothered me a little.

"Mmhm." He nodded his head as I took his small hand into mine.

"Mommy and Nas aren't friends anymore." We walked side by side up the snowy walkway.

"Why?"

"Because Mommy doesn't like him," I lied.

"Why?"

"Because he makes me mad."

"Why?"

"Bean..." I groaned. He had clearly been hanging around his cousins and Auntie Jade too much. Just nosey.

My nerves were all over the place as I approached Troy's home. I knew I shouldn't just pop up, but he hadn't reached out to Duke in almost two weeks. Imagine my surprise when I got a knock on my front door at five in the morning only to come face to face with a complete stranger, dropping off gifts like Santa Claus. And to be honest, that's why my Christmas had been shitty so far. Maybe that's why Duke was getting under my skin so easily. I needed a blunt bad.

Coming up the massive, wide double doors to his home, I stopped to make sure Duke looked presentable. Fixing his coat one more time, I rang the doorbell.

"I don't want to see my daddy," Duke pouted. "I wanna go home," he whined.

"Bean, please." I looked down at my baby. "You don't want to say Merry Christmas to your dad?"

He shook his head no.

Well too bad. Cause he got me fucked up.

We waited for someone to come to the door.

"I'm going to Nas' house," he told me with his mind made up.

The hell you are.

Hearing the locks on the door pop made me stand up straight and clear my throat.

"Honey, it's probably just Isa—" Troy's wife, Nina, stopped mid-sentence and looked me up and down.

"I need to speak with Troy." I looked down at Duke quickly then back to her.

"He's busy." She mugged me. "With his family."

"That's perfect." I smiled. "Duke needs to speak with him as well."

She crossed her arms across her chest. "How dare you come to my home, little girl? Parading your child around, proud that you slept with a married man." Looking down at Duke, she sighed.

"Nina." I shook my head in annoyance. "I probably hate more than you that Troy is the father of my child." The cold air whipped across my face, reminding me it was below zero. "Go get him." I pulled Duke closer to me.

"I will not." She looked appalled. "We have relatives coming and—"

"Honey, what's taking you so long?" Troy asked as he neared the door. Our eyes connected and he looked shocked.

"Troy, I need to talk to you *now*."

"Excuse you," she butted in.

"Honey, give me a second, okay?" he spoke to her, but he kept his eyes on me.

"What?! We have family coming at any moment and you're going to invite your mistress in on Christmas?!"

I sighed. Nina had more time. One. I didn't want to act rowdy in front Duke, but she was pressing all the right buttons.

"Honey, five minutes, okay?" He kissed her forehead. "Five minutes."

She stared back and forth between Troy and me before she finally gave up. "Three minutes, Troy Warren and then I want them out." Spinning on her heels, she walked away, mumbling profanities.

"Come in." Troy ushered. "Get out of that cold." He smiled as we entered. "Merry Christmas, son." He patted the top of Duke's head.

"Merry Christmas."

"Did you guys like your gifts?" He had the nerve to try to pull me in for a hug.

I stiffed armed his ass so fast. "Troy, you couldn't have dropped them off on your own?"

He sighed. "Meme, come on." He groaned. "It's Christmas. Can you drop the attitude at least for today?"

"Why can't you treat Duke the same way you treat the kids you live with? Huh? Because he's the side baby?" I stepped closer to him. "Huh? Or is it because he's not mixed like your other children?"

"Now, Jaime," he snapped sternly.

"No." I poked him hard in the chest. "How is it that your white wife can take black dick, but can't stand black *people*?"

"That's not—"

"I told you to man up a long time ago."

"Do you really want to do this now? Here? In front of our son?" he asked in disbelief.

"I sure the fuck do. Duke needs you just as much as your other kids do."

"He has me."

"*Part-time!*" I exploded. "He has you part-time. I get that you're a busy man, but to have another man drop off Christmas gifts to your son for you is low and pathetic."

"Meme..." He sighed.

"We may not be as rich as you, privileged as you, as articulate as you, but we're human and we have feelings, Troy." I pointed at Duke. "Your son has feelings."

"I know that."

"Act like it."

"It's complicated, Jaime, and you *know* that."

"You're *making* it complicated."

"Troy..." That was Nina's hating ass. "Don't you think you should be wrapping it up?"

"Nina, hun, give me a second."

"I gave you three minutes."

"Nina, I came to talk to Troy."

" I don't care."

"Okay, hold on." Troy stood in between us. "Meme, I'll call you later to finish this conversation."

"After I leave here, the conversation will already be finished. I won't pressure or beg you to be a father to your son ever again."

"Now, wait a minute."

I ignored him and opened the door. "Let's go, Bean."

"Jaime!"

"No, let them go."

Exiting, I picked Duke up, practically running to my Jeep. "You ready to go see Auntie Jade?"

"Jaime!" Troy rushed behind us. "Why are you doing this? Don't I provide everything you and Duke could possibly need?"

Still, I ignored him.

"Who is Nas, Jaime?"

That question made me stop in my tracks. Turning to face him, I adjusted Duke on my hip. "What?"

"Nas? Who is that?"

"None of your business." I started for my ride again.

"Anyone who keeps my son without my permission is my business," he snapped as I opened the back door to put Duke inside. "Is he the man I heard in your background when we were in California."

I ignored him.

"Answer me!"

I shut the door and made my way to the driver's side.

"Are you sleeping with him?" His voice softened. "Please tell me you aren't sleeping with him, Jaime Desirae."

Oh...he's in his feeling.

He had to be. For him to be saying my middle name.

Opening my door, I tossed my purse in the passenger's seat. Amused. "Wouldn't you like to know?"

"You are, aren't you?" The pout he gave was one of a toddler who couldn't have his way.

Hopping inside, I started the ignition and pulled my seatbelt across my body. "You should be more worried about your son."

"I am worried about my son. So when he tells me some man named Nas took him to hang around a man named Kai Money, it raises red flags, Meme. Are these street dudes?"

"Can you please shut my door, Troy?" Agitated, I looked through my rearview to see what Duke was doing.

"Is that the kind of life you want for our son?"

"Shut my door!" I damn near yelled as my phone started ringing. Snatching it up, I rolled my eyes.

Speak of the devil.

"I'll let you go for now, Jaime, but this isn't over."

***

"Thank you Auntie Meme." Shane hugged me tight.

"You're welcome" I kissed her forehead.

"Meme, you wanna babysit for me tonight?" Jade asked, rolling up a joint. "It's this Christmas party in Jersey I'm trying to hit up."

I shrugged.

"Bet. Can I borrow your Jeep?"

She tried it.

"My Jeep? Hell no, Jade. What's wrong with your car?"

"Nothing. Your Jeep is bigger and Myeisha and her home girls are trying to ride out with me." She licked the shell, sealing it close.

"I don't know about all that." Jade and her home girls always did the most. They were always in the middle of some drama.

"Come on, Meme. It's only for a couple hours. We can swap rides. I aint tryna be all bunched up during the ride to Jersey."

"Jay—"

My phone went off. Noticing Nasir was calling me yet *again*, I figured something must've been wrong. Lifting my finger, I asked Jade to hold on.

"Hello?"

"Yo, Jaime, you ain't seen me calling you all morning?" He told somebody to hold up.

"What did you want? Didn't you say you were done with me?" It was nice hearing his voice. I actually smiled a little.

"I am done with your bipolar ass."

I rolled my eyes. "So, what do you want?"

"I wanna talk to my guy."

I looked over at Duke who was playing PlayStation with Armond. "About?"

"Just put Duke on the phone, man," he ordered in his rough, raspy voice. "Why I gotta always tell you to do shit more than once?" He had the nerve to try and check me.

Putting my phone on speaker, I told Duke to come here. "Say hello." I handed him the phone.

"Hello?" asked uninterested.

"Duke, my guy. Merry Christmas, dude."

Duke's entire face lit up. "What's up, Nas?"

Jade lit the blunt and passed it to me giving me the side eye.

"What did you get?"

"My mama got me some clothes and toys. Auntie Jade got me some clothes and my dad was yelling at my mama."

I almost choked on the smoke I'd just inhaled. Coughing, I took my phone out of his hand and passed the joint back to Jade.

"He—" I cleared my throat. "Hello?"

"Why the fuck that nigga yelling at you, Jaime?" Nas, who was still on speaker, shouted.

"He wasn't yelling at me, Nas."

"So, you're calling Duke a liar?" he pressed.

"Nas..." I almost whined. I didn't feel like arguing with him.

"Nah, don't Nas me, yo. Put Duke back on the phone."

Sighing, I handed Duke the phone again.

"Meme, quit letting him run you." Jade rolled her eyes.

"Shut yo hoe ass up." Nas' voice blared through the speaker.

"Ugh." She stood up. "I can't stand his ass." Storming off, she made her way to the kitchen.

"Nas?" Duke said.

"Yeah, man. I'ma see you later. A'ight?"

"A'ight." Duke tried to sound like him.

"Don't be giving your moms a hard time either." He chuckled.

Duke giggled. "A'ight."

"Put your mama on the phone."

Taking the phone from him I took it off speaker.

"Yeah?"

"Why was that nigga yelling at you?"

"I went over to talk and it escalated. It's not that serious." I reached for my bottle of water.

"Yeah, a'ight." He sucked his teeth. "Yo, Tami, get outta my face, man. You see I'm on the phone."

Tami?

"Who is Tami?" The question left my lips before I could stop it. Who the fuck was Tami and why was Nas spending Christmas with her? Was she his woman? That's when it dawned on me that I'd never asked if he was seeing anyone.

"My peoples."

I frowned. "Your peoples?"

"Mmhm. Aye, when you leave that slut's house, slide through. I got something for my guy."

"Slide through where?" I asked, looking at Duke.

"My spot. I'm bout to send you the address now. Matter of fact, come on now while I'm sitting still so I won't miss ya'll." He demanded.

"You want me to come while *Tami* is there?" I was in my feelings.

"Jaime, bring yo ass." With that, he hung up in my face.

Nas

"Nas, some chick and a little boy is at your door." My sister Nikki rounded the corner entering the room.

Following her to the front of my crib, I mentally prepared myself for the slick-ass remarks I knew Jaime was about to make. Even though her lil' ass was sometimey, I was hyped as fuck she had actually pulled up.

"Who is she, Nas?" Tami, who was sitting on my couch with a personal bottle of Cîroc asked.

"Don't trip. And I don't want no bullshit from either one of ya'll." I stared back and forth between Nikki and her side kick.

"So, you playing step daddy now?" Nikki rolled her eyes.

Ignoring her I kept on down the hallway and to the front door.

"Duke, my guy." He gave me a quick pound as I let them in.

"What's up, Nas?" He cheesed, walking past me and towards the living room.

"Duke, you can't just be walking through people's houses." Jaime was starting already.

"Shut up," I said smacking her hard on the ass as I shut the door.

"Ouch, Nas. That hurt." She frowned, rubbing her butt.

"I don't see how. That muthafucka's phat as fuck." I smacked her ass again. "And you overdue for a whoopin' anyway."

She snickered.

"Come on." I led the way to the living room. We barely made it past the threshold when Tami spoke up.

"Who is she?" her hardheaded ass asked.

"Yo, what the fuck did I say?" I gave her a hard stare. "Mind your business or take yo ass on. You too." My gaze shifted to Nikki.

"See?" Nikki stood up. "Rude-ass nigga. Come on, Tam, help me get this food together so we can go."

At first Tami didn't budge.

"Bye." I waved her dumb ass off, taking a seat on my sectional.

After she left, Jaime sighed loudly.

"What you huffing and puffing for?" It was too many attitudes in one spot.

"Can you give Duke what you have for him so we can go?" She crossed her arms over her chest.

"Sit down."

"We're not staying long."

"What did I say? You complain about Duke never listening, but he gets it from you. Sit down and be quiet." I stood up and made my way to the Christmas tree.

Like I knew she would, she stayed in the same spot.

This girl.

"Nas, is this one mine?" Duke asked, holding up a big box wrapped in Superman gift paper thanks to Blaze.

"Yeah, all of those are." I reached under the tree for Jaime's gift. "Go head and open em." I stepped back to let him do his thing. "Here." I handed Jaime her shit before I took off towards the kitchen.

"Nas, who is she to you?" Tami asked me as I opened the door to the garage.

Stepping inside, I went for the Maybach power wheel I'd gotten Duke. Pushing it through the kitchen past Nikki and Tami, I made my way back to the living room. Duke dropped everything in his small hands and ran towards me.

"Oooooh!" He clapped, excited. "Mama, look at my car." He cheesed, hopping inside.

"Every man needs his own whip." I smiled proudly. "Look." I bent down to his level. "You got an MP3 player in it and everything. Yo shit bump too." I picked a Meek Mill joint and it started blasting throughout the car.

Duke bobbed his head coolly, making me and Jaime laugh.

"Can I let my seat back like yours?"he asked.

I chuckled.

Jaime snickered.

"You can't even drive yet. What you need to lean back for?" I asked, handing Jaime the remote control to it. "Put your feet on the gas." I helped him.

We watched as he maneuvered slowly through the open space.

"He needs to be outside with that. I don't want him to break anything in here." Jaime started hating.

"Let the lil' nigga live. He good. It's plenty of space for him to ride it in the house. Plus it's cold outside." I faced her sexy ass. "Open your shit."

"My shit?" she laughed. "I didn't get you a gift." She looked down at the small gift bag.

"You and Duke being here is my gift, shorty." I couldn't even believe I had said that corny shit. But I meant it and I felt that shit too.

Damn.

Jaime looked off bashfully.

"Open it, so I can see how it looks on you." Licking my lips, I eyed her. Everything in me wanted to carry Jaime upstairs and break her back in. A nigga would even settle for a just a taste of the pussy.

Yeah, Jaime was trouble.

She smiled as she rummaged through the bag until she pulled out a jewelry box. Lifting the lid, she cheesed, shaking her head. "Really?" She laughed, taking the necklace out of the box.

I chuckled. "Fuck yeah."

"Put it on me." Handing it over to me, she lifted her hair and turned her back to me.

After securing the back, I grabbed a handful of her hair and pulled her head back gently. Kissing the side of her neck, I whispered in her ear. "And don't take this muthafucka off either."

Running her index finger across the gold and diamond *Nas* pendent hanging from the gold chain, she shook her head, smiling. "What I'ma do wit' you?"

Chapter Eight

Love on the brain…

Jaime

"Auntie Meme!" My niece Maxx ran towards me full speed.

"Hey, Maxxie!" I laughed as she jumped into my arms. "I missed you."

"I missed you too, girl." She held on to me tighter.

I snickered at her little grown ass.

"Sister!" Jaylen's silly ass hugged me from behind. "Oh, how I've missed you, my love,she sang playfully in my ear.

I cheesed, shaking my head at the both of them. When we finally let go of one another, I looked my baby sister over and smiled proudly. She was the spitting image of our mother with the same toffee skin, long and pretty hair, and small beauty mark on her chin. Jaylen shared the same eyes Jade and I had, but hers always seemed to be more youthful.

"So where's my brother-in-law?" She looked around. "I know he got a friend for me."

Rolling my eyes, I grabbed Maxx's luggage. "He's not your brother-in-law." I'd told Len about Nas' Christmas gift and now, she was dead set on him being my soul mate. She was weird and believed in shit like that.

Waving me off, she led the way through the airport. "Girl, tell that to somebody who don't know you."

"Apparently, you don't know me that well," I shot back.

"Maybe I don't." She shrugged. "But what I *do* know is you can't fool me."

Honestly, I didn't know how to feel about me and Nas' *situationship*. Ever since Christmas two days ago, he'd been spending the night...*every* night. The sex was mindblowing and bomb as fuck. Not only did he tend to my every need, but Duke's as well. He'd even had the nerve to catch an attitude when I told him he couldn't spend the night because Maxx and Jaylen were coming to town, whining and complaining the entire ride to the airport.

"Where's Duke?" Maxx asked, sliding her small hand into mine.

"He's in the car," I told her, tightening our grasp.

"With who?" She bounced along next to me, holding her American Doll, who was dressed exactly like her.

"His step daddy," Jaylen answered sniggling. I poked her in the back hard and she burst into a fit of laughter. "Don't be hitting me."

We made it outside and I led the way to Nas' red G-wagon. He was posted against the passenger's door, talking to Duke who was hanging out of the passenger's window eating hot chips.

"Mama, that's Duke's step daddy?" Maxx asked, letting go of my hand.

"No," I answered as we came up on his SUV.

"Dukie!" Jaylen exclaimed, sitting her luggage down on the ground.

Nas moved over so she could open the door. "Don't be calling my lil' nigga Dukie, man," he fussed.

"Oh hush, brother-in-law." Jaylen giggled, pulling Duke into her arms. "Hey, Dukie, I missed you."

Nas chuckled.

"You smell like baby powder. Tell your mama you ain't no damn baby no more," she joked, letting him go.

"Auntie Len, I got a car." He cheesed, looking to Nas proudly.

"No, you don't. You too small for a car," Maxx interrupted

"Shut up, ugly."

"Duke." I gave him a stern look.

"Leave him alone." Nas opened the passenger's door for me. "Hop in the back, dude," he addressed Duke, who wasted no time doing what he was told.

So, this is the infamous *Nasir*." Jaylen studied Nas, looking his tall frame up and down.

"In the flesh." Nas smirked, chewing on a piece of gum.

"You love my sister, huh?" She cheesed.

"Jaylen, for real?" Opening the back door, I slid Maxx's luggage across the seat and then helped her climb in. "Put your seatbelt on, Maxxie."

"Kay."

"I can't joke around with my brother-in-law?" She laughed as I stepped to the side, giving her room to get in.

"You know she's sensitive." Nas slapped me hard on the butt.

"Really?" I glared at him. I'd been telling his heavy-handed ass to stop doing that.

"Shut up and get in the car," he said, holding on to my door.

Jaylen snickered, hopping inside. "Ya'll so damn cute," she leaned forward to tell me as Nas shut my door and made his way around to the driver's side.

***

"I'ma get wit' you later, a'ight?"

I nodded my head in response as I watched Jaylen and Maxx make their way up the steps to my brownstone.

"Nas, can I go wit' you?" Duke's little hardheaded ass asked from the back seat. I'd told him to go in the house with Jaylen, yet somehow, he managed to still be seated comfortably in his booster seat.

"Ask your mama," Nas said, handing me some cash.

"Mama, can I go?"

"What's this for?" I asked as I started counting it.

"Whatever you need it for. Gimme a kiss."

I stopped counting once I got to twelve hundred and I wasn't even half way through the stack. Leaning over I planted a wet kiss on his lips, and he slid his tongue in my mouth. Gripping my chin, Nas pulled me closer, running his left hand up the inside of my thigh. Immediately, my pussy got wet. My eyes were still closed when he pulled away and chuckled lightly.

Opening them slowly, I licked my lips and eyed him hungrily.

"Mama..." I could hear the pout in Duke's voice. "I wanna go."

"Du—"

"Aye, man," Nas cut me off. "What I say about that whining shit?" He turned in his seat to look at Duke, who sat up straight in his booster seat. "Cut that out. You ain't no girl."

"Okay." Duke looked to me, apparently, still awaiting my answer.

"Bean, you don't want to go to Auntie Jade's?"

"No. I wanna go wit' Nas," he said in finality, grabbing his soda from the seat next to him and handing it to Nas.

Taking it from him, Nas opened it and passed it back.

"Where are you going?" I addressed Nas, but I kept my gaze on Duke.

"Shit around. Turn a few corners, see what the family got up." He shrugged, stroking his beard. "Why? You wanna come too?"

"No, I told you my dad is at Jade's so we can talk to him."

He nodded. "Even more reason for my guy to ride out wit' me. He don't need to be around all that. I already told you I don't like you hanging over there anyway."

I sighed.

"I don't care about that attitude. Why can't they come over here?"

"I don't know. We usually just all go to Jade's since he lives with her."

"Well, I don't want you over on that side." A notification from his phone came through. Picking it up, he scrolled through his messages.

"I can see if she can get him to come." I guess good dick made you obedient because if Nas didn't want me in the Bronx, then I wasn't going.

"Sounds like a plan to me," he spoke, looking down at his phone.

"What time will you be back?" All of a sudden, I was feeling real clingy.

Ew.

I sighed.

"Before ten. I don't want Duke out that late." His eyes were still on his phone. Whoever had texted him now had his undivided attention.

"Okay." I opened my door. "I love you, Bean. Be good, okay?"

"Okay." He cheesed

I hopped out of Nas' G-Wagon with an attitude. Who the fuck was he texting? I was getting ready to shut my door, when finally he looked up and over at me.

"I don't get no bye?" He smirked. "What you frowning for?"

"I ain't tripping." I played it off or at least I tried to. We weren't even in that stage of our relationship for me to be jealous. Hell, I didn't even know where we stood with one another. Technically, we were both still single.

"Yeah, a'ight. Answer the phone when I call."

I might.

Slamming the door shut, I made my way up the stairs and to my front door. Once it was open, I heard Nas' stereo before he pulled off down that street.

COVERED IN YOUR LOVE 2
by *Nique Luarks*

Ryan

Entering the Queens Center, I headed for the food court in search of Blaze. I only had one more day in New York and I would be spending it shopping and pampering myself with my girl. The moment I stepped into the building, a wide smile spread across my face. This was home. Not the mall but the atmosphere. And even though I hated to admit it, I missed the hell out of it.

It was busy as usual as I made my way through the crowd. Finally, coming up on the food court, I scanned the sitting area looking for Blaze. When my eyes landed on Kenya, my smile widened. Making my way over to her, I almost stopped in my tracks when I saw who she was sitting next to. Instantly, my smile left my face and I rolled my eyes in annoyance.

"Ry!" Kenya jumped out of her seat when she noticed me. "Bitch!" She grinned.

I chuckled. "What's up, Ken—"

"Bitch, you. Where you been?" She laughed, pulling me into a hug.

"Around."

"Mmhm...I didn't invite Ava," she spoke lowly. "You know that was all *Mother Hen's* idea."

I laughed. Of course it was. That was Blaze. Always trying to find a solution to everybody's problems. I would never knock her for that. I couldn't even be mad because I knew her intentions were good.

As I approached the table, I still didn't see Blaze. Ava however, stared me up and down.

"What, you got a staring problem?" I asked, sitting across from her.

She chuckled lightly. "It's good to see you too, Ryan."

"So..." Kenya started. "How long do ya'll plan on being mad at each other?" Picking her burger up, she took a big bite. "I know ya'll ain't about to let this petty shit come between ya'll." She smacked.

"I'm not mad at Ry. She's buggin'." Ava rolled her eyes, picking at her fries.

Kenya stared at me.

"What?" I stared back.

"Can ya'll just make up?" Kenya asked, agitated.

"I'm not worried about you, Ava. I promise. I'm cool on you, though."

Kenya sighed and took a sip from her cup.

"Where's Blaze?" I was over the conversation.

"Here she comes now." Kenya pointed.

When my eyes landed on Blaze, I smiled again.

"Hey, Ry!"

I stood up to give her a hug. "Hey, B." Letting her go, I looked down at Ava. "I didn't know you invited ya girl."

Ava chuckled and Kenya shook her head.

"It was last minute. Did you ladies catch up?" Blaze took a seat next to Ava.

"Yo,Blaze, really?" I caught an instant attitude. "You know I don't fuck with her." I continued standing, because I was ready leave.

"How did you forgive Quan but not me?" Ava crossed her arms over her chest. "I'm not understanding."

"It's not for you to understand." I glared at her. How did she even know I'd seen him?

"Well, I want to," she shot back. "What? You wanna fight?" She stood up.

"Ah, shit." Kenya sucked her teeth.

"No, ya'll, come on." Blaze sighed.

"Ava, I will beat yo ass." I sat my purse down on the table.

She smirked. "It won't be easy."

Running my tongue across my top row of teeth, I looked her up and down.

"Plus, you know I'm not good at taking losses. Bitch, I will do you like I did that hoe, Tamika."

I tried to keep a straight face when she said that. Ava wasn't really a fighter, but she'd tase a bitch with the quickness. Tamika didn't even see it coming when Ava's crazy ass tased her at a damn birthday party. Had kids screaming and crying everywhere. Her ass didn't stop until Tamika shitted on herself and passed out. Nas was pissed when he came with Quan to bail us out of jail.

"They will carry you out this bitch, stankin'." She snickered.

I pressed my lips together to keep from laughing. The images of Tamika laid out on the floor with her kids surrounding her flashed across my mind. All because she had called Ava's crazy ass a stupid bitch on Facebook.

"Now, give me hug and get out yo feelings." She grinned, approaching me with her arms outstretched wide.

Shaking my head, I rolled my eyes.

"Don't be acting like that. You know you missed me." She pulled me in. "I had to go to jail all by myself last week."

I couldn't even hold my smile in after that. Crazy ass. Giving in, I wrapped my arms around her sluggishly.

"I sure did miss you, Keyshia."

I laughed, pulling away from her.

"So, you back with Quan, huh?" She retook her seat next to Blaze. "Umhm, I called him to tell him Kai had some work for him and imagine my surprise when I hear *My Ry* in the back telling him she can't feel her legs." She sipped from her straw, giving me a knowing look.

Kenya burst into a fit of laughter. "Damn."

Blaze giggled, shaking her head bashfully.

"That's why you don't wanna leave his ass alone. He paralyzing you and shit." Ava snickered. "I wouldn't leave either."

We all shared a hearty laugh.

Sitting down next to Kenya, I shook my head. "I'm not back with Quan," I clarified.

Ava rolled her eyes. "C'mon, Ry. I ain't judging. I'm just saying. You know ya'll can't stay apart." She picked up a fry, stuck it in her mouth, and chewed dramatically. "I'm surprised you been gone this long."

I now had everybody's anxious eyes on me. Sighing, I looked back and forth between my girls. I could easily tell them I was in a vulnerable, drunk state or I could lie and say that night with Quan meant absolutely nothing to me. Because even though I was indeed drunk *and* vulnerable, the moment I sobered up and we parted ways, I was reminded he was and would always be my first everything.

But there was nothing we could do to salvage our relationship at this point. He'd taken it too far bringing a baby into the equation. How could I compare to that? I couldn't, I shouldn't, and I damn sure wouldn't. He'd given her what I'd been wanting for a while—a family. And then he gave it to our biggest headache.

Sitting my phone down, I sighed. "Even if I wanted to be with DaQuan, it would never work. The damage is done."

Kenya nodded.

"Because of the baby?" Blaze asked.

Ava smacked her lips. "Fuck that baby."

"Ava." Blaze cringed. "Really? The baby?"

"Hell yeah."

Kenya laughed. "This bitch."

"What? I'm just saying. Quan don't want a damn baby with that basic-ass bitch. How we even know it's his? Because she said?" Sucking her teeth, she picked up her cup. "Ry, you and I know how Brianna and her home girls get down."

Kenya snickered.

"The fact that he's claiming her baby is enough for me." I shrugged. I wasn't cut out to be anybody's step mama. I didn't even have kids of my own, so why should I have to play mama to the next bitch's kids?

"So, you can really sit here and say with a straight face that you're done with Quan?" Ava pressed.

"No, I could never be *done* with him," I spoke truthfully. "I share too much of my past and pain with him."

"So, ya'll basically just fucked for the road?" Kenya probed.

"Basically."

"Yeah, a'ight." Ava stared at me like she knew something I didn't.

"Plus, it ain't like I won't ever see him when I come to visit. Considering the fact that he's connected to ya'll in some way, I'm bound to run into him."

"So, you gon' fuck him every time you visit?" Kenya looked amused. "Might as well."

I chuckled. "Nah, that was it."

Ava shrugged. "Oh well, we can flaunt you around and show him how big of a loss he took."

Blaze giggled. "It really is his loss, though. He only pushed you to be a better you anyway."

I smiled. "Yeah, you right. School has been taking up a lot of my spare time."

Ava damn near jumped out of her chair. "School bitch!" We slapped fives. "Yaaaas, bitch! That's what the fuck I'm talkin' bout." She grinned.

I nodded. "Yeah, I figured if I'm going to go to school, I might as well go for something I'm good at doing."

Ava cheesed. "Makeup."

"Yep."

"That's what' up. So, you know we gotta celebrate." She grinned mischievously, rubbing her hands together.

I frowned.

Kenya stood up. "Good thing we at the mall then. I can find something to wear right quick."

"All them damn clothes you have. You and Cole have a problem." Blaze stood up too, grabbing her Louie bag.

"I didn't agree to go out." I looked up at all three of them as Ava got up.

"You didn't have to." Ava snatched up her keys and phone. "Drinks on the men tonight." She held up a black card. "The shopping spree is too."

Chapter Nine

We got something special

Nas

"Daddy, Duke won't let me play his iPad." Tatianna, Cole's daughter ran into the room pouting. The big puff balls on the top of her hair bounced as she plopped down into his lap.

"Quit snitchin'." He took a pull from the blunt in his hand. "You got a phone anyway. Where is it?" He put the joint out.

"He is bad, Daddy. He just told Nana Haley to shut the F-word up," she said, referring to the nanny Kai Money and Blaze had hired to look after the twins. She turned to me. "Can you tell your bad son to let me see his iPad?"

Before I could respond to her, my phone went off. Answering the FaceTime from Jaime, I called out for Duke.

"Yo."

"Hey, where's Duke?" She looked like she'd been crying.

"Right here." Looking up from my phone, I watched Duke run into the room.

"Huh?" He came to my side. Handing him my phone, he cheesed when he saw it was his mama.

"Hi, Bean?" she sniffled. "You being good for Nasir?"

"Yep." He leaned back against me.

"No, he ain't," Tati cut in, hopping off her daddy's lap. Standing next to Duke, she peered into the FaceTime.

Jaime chuckled. "Hi, pretty girl."

"Hi. Your son is bad." Her lil' six-year-old ass going on twenty-six said, rolling her neck. I was sure she'd gotten that shit from her ghetto-ass mama.

"Yo, Tati." Cole sighed.

"I'm not bad." Duke scrunched his face up. "Shut up."

"You don't miss me, Bean?" Jaime wiped her nose with a Kleenex.

"Mmhm," he mumbled, looking down at his iPad.

"Can I see your son's iPad?" Tati tried to take my phone out of Duke's hand, but he snatched away from her.

"Sure. Duke, you wanna let the pretty girl play with you?" I could see Jaime walking down what looked to be a dimly-lit hallway.

"No," he answered, still looking down at the game he was playing.

by *Nique Luarks*

Staring at Jaime's red, watery eyes, I got annoyed. "What the fuck you crying for?"

She sighed and didn't answer me. Instead, she paused the FaceTime and then I could hear her turn on the faucet. Leaning forward in my seat, I waited for her to come back on. When she did, he bright eyes looked doleful. My heart rate sped up. Somebody was about to die.

"Why you crying?"

"I think I'm getting sick," she lied right to my face.

"Where you at?" Standing up, I hit my boys with a quick nod and started for the exit. "Let's go, Duke." I kept on towards the front of Kai's crib.

"I'm at home chilling with Jaylen." She sniffled again. "You can bring Duke whenever you're ready. My dad and Jade are gone."

I nodded, removing Duke's coats and mine out of the hall closet. "We on our way."

***

Jaime's front door was already unlocked, which pissed me off even more as Duke led the way inside. I followed him through the brownstone until we reached the kitchen where I heard someone humming. I stood at the threshold watching Jaime wash dishes, bobbing her head swiftly to whatever sounds were spilling from her Beats headphones. Wearing only a black sports bra and black leggings, I admired her curvy frame and the tattoos covering her entire back. Absentmindedly, I grabbed the bulge in my pants, licking my lips.

"Mama!" Duke ran to her, wrapping his arms around her thick thigh.

"Shit!" She jumped in fear. "Bean, you scared me." She laughed, taking her headphones off.

Facing me, she tried to brighten her smile, but I saw through the bullshit. Resting my back against the doorjamb, I looked her over slowly and carefully.

"Come here, Jaime."

Duke ran past me and out of the kitchen.

"Was he good? I know how hard-headed he can be." She sighed, drying off her hands and then trekking in my direction.

"He straight." When she stopped in front of me, I gripped her hips and pulled her closer. "Why the fuck you been crying?"

"It's just a lot going on with my dad." Her lip trembled. "He won't let us help him."

COVERED IN YOUR LOVE 2
by *Nique Luarks*

I sighed deeply. I wanted to tell my lil' baby she was wasting her tears and her time. Her pops was a full-fledged junkie. The only people who could help him now were doctors and nurses. He was too far gone, and I honestly didn't want her dealing with him. Dope heads weren't to be trusted. I'd watched firsthand the things they'd do to their own families all for a quick fix.

But I couldn't tell her that because she was already hurting. I opted out of the harsh truth and decided I'd sugar coat some shit for her. Gripping her thighs, I picked her up and carried her to the counter. Sitting her down, I stood between her legs and kissed her neck. I'd never been the type of nigga to think before I speak. But for my lil' baby I was willing to give it a try.

"So, what happened?"

She stared off into space, shaking her head. "Jade pretty much ruined the whole conversation. They started arguing." She sighed. "He said some very hurtful things and then he stormed out. After he threw the lamp from my end table at the wall."

Clenching my jaw, I nodded.

"Then Jaylen and Jade damn near came to blows."

Immediately. I noticed the scratches on her neck and arms. "They did this?" I asked, running my finger across the welts on her smooth chocolate skin.

"Jade did most of it. She was really trying to get at Len like she was some bitch off the streets. It's like she forgot that we're blood related," she vented, visibly annoyed.

"I told you I don't like that sneaky muthafucka."

"Nas…" she groaned. "Not right now."

"Yeah…a'ight." I pulled her closer to the edge of the counter. "What can I do?"

She gave me a confused look. "What?"

"What can I do to make you feel better?"

She blushed. Her little cheeks turned a shade lighter. Biting down her on juicy, shiny bottom lip, she gazed up at me. "I'm okay, really. I just wasn't expecting it to turn out that way."

"A'ight." I leaned forward to kiss her lips.

"Mama." Duke barged in, making me pull away. "I'm hungry."

I picked Jaime up and she wrapped her legs around my waist. Duke giggled.

"You ain't no baby, Mama." He laughed, following close behind me as I made my way down the hallway.

Jaime snickered. "Tell him again, Bean."

"I'm my mama's baby." He hopped playfully up the stairs, now leading the way.

"And your mama is *my* baby." I bit down on her neck softly.

"We going to get something to eat?" he asked, picking up a toy that was at the very top of the steps.

"Yeah, after your mama puts some clothes on." I continued carrying Jaime to her room as Duke rushed towards his room.

"Don't forget to take your shoes off," she stressed.

"Shut up." Pinching her ass, I stepped into her room and shut the door behind us.

Jaime

"You can put me down now." I smiled, shaking my head.

"I'm bout to." Nas carried me to my bed and laid me down. Kissing my collar bone, he tugged at my leggings.

"Nas..." I tried to pull them back up. "Duke and Jaylen are in the next room," I reminded him. We usually only had sex when Duke was asleep. I didn't want my son to hear me calling out for God.

"So what?" His tongue snaked up my neck.

"Mmmm.. I moaned as our mouths connected. Nas had to have the softest lips I'd ever kissed.

I was so lost in our kiss that I forgot all about him trying to strip me naked until I felt a cool breeze hit my vagina.

"You were waiting on Daddy, huh?" He smirked, causing me to look away shyly. I'd gotten out of the shower and decided against underwear.

Hearing his zipper made me face him again.

"I was thinking about this pussy all day." He eyed me seductively. Stroking his manhood, he slapped my bare thigh. "Turn over."

Quickly getting on all fours, I bent over, poking my ass in the air.

Knock, knock.

"Nas, I got my coat on." Duke spoke on the other side of the door.

Shit.

Shaking my head, I tried to move away from Nas, but he pulled me back by my hips and slapped me hard on the ass.

"I ain't tell you to move," he mumbled, sliding his dick into me slowly.

"Mmmm…" Closing my eyes, I bit down on the corner of my lip. Scooting back some, I helped him fill me up.

Knock, knock.

"Mama..."

"Shit," I whimpered.

"Damn," he groaned lowly, spreading my ass cheeks apart. "Tight-ass pussy."

Our strokes were in sync as we fucked each other hard.

"Oh my God," I groaned, panting and dropping my face onto my bed. "Please don't stop. Right there, baby."

"You cumming for Daddy, huh?"

"Yessss."

"Come on this muthafucka then. It's yours." He pumped faster, harder, deeper.

"Nassss, I'm cumming." I hollered, digging my nails into my comforter.

"I feel you, baby." He kept his pace, squeezing two handfuls of my ass.

"I feel you too, Daddy. You in my stomach, Nas." I surrendered to my orgasm. My body bucked as I came, but he didn't slow up.

"I'm in yo stomach, huh?" he growled, leaning forward, thrusting into me harder. Moving his pelvis in a circular motion, he pulled my head back by my ponytail.

"Yesss." I couldn't even keep my eyes straight, so I closed them tight as I rode another orgasmic wave.

Jesus.

"Where you want Daddy nut at?" he growled in a low, raspy voice. "You want Daddy to cum in this pussy."

His strokes deepened.

"Yes." Hell, I'd take that risk and give Nas twenty babies as long as he always fucked me like *this*.

by *Nique Luarks*

"Fuuuck," he groaned and stopped stroking. Gripping my waist so I would stay still, I could feel his dick pulsating inside of me.

Twerking my butt, I rode his dick, milking him for everything he had.

"Jaime...Ma..." He tried to keep me still.

When I wouldn't stop, he slipped out of me, still groaning.

Knock, knock.

"Nas, Mama, I'm hungry."

Immediately, I felt guilty for having Duke out there banging on the door, saying he was hungry.

"Here we come, Duke," Nas answered him, pulling his pants up.

"Okay!" Duke's small voice bounced off the door.

Falling on my side, I laid my head down and prepared to close my eyes. That was until Nas' heavy-handed ass smacked me on the butt.

"Get up and get dressed. You heard my guy. He's hungry."

"I'm coming." I muttered, looking up at him lustfully.

Knock, knock.

"Mama!"

"Okay, Bean," I spoke loud enough for him to hear me.

"Hurry up." He had grown impatient.

Nas chuckled, heading towards the door. "Get yo ass up, short stuff. Both of your boys are starving, son." He rubbed his stomach.

I quickly threw some of my cover over the bottom half of my body.

"I said I'm coming," I grumbled. Annoyed because I'd rather take a nap. My pussy felt worn out and all I wanted to do was fall into a deep slumber. But I was a Mommy first and I had a child to feed.

Damn it, Nas.

Chapter Ten

While we're young

Ryan

Looking at myself in the full-length mirror located in Blaze's massive guest room, I combed through my hair. Even though I'd been wearing sew-ins, my real hair stayed treated. There were no split ends and it was now reaching the top of my shoulders. The silk press I'd had done before I came to New York still looked fresh, bouncy, and full. Fixing my feathered bang to my liking, I turned sideways to give my outfit approval too.

The leather off-the-shoulder jacket hugged me tight, making me notice just how much weight I'd lost. My collar bone had always been noticeable, but now it was more defined. The bright tattoos on my shoulders and upper arms popped, giving me a sexy biker-chick look. I paired the jacket with black ripped Givenchy jeans and black thigh-high boots. I'd chosen to keep my makeup subtle to give me a softer look.

"Ry, you ready?" Blaze knocked softly on the already cracked door, and poked her head in.

"Yeah, let me get my clutch." I went towards the mahogany dresser.

"Cool, Kenya and Ava are downstairs already." She then walked away.

With my clutch in hand, I made sure I had my lip-gloss, cut the lights out and headed downstairs. Kai Money really had his little family living like royals. The high ceilings and white, grey and black decor was mad dope. I'm not sure how many rooms it held, but I knew it was equipped with a full movie theatre, bowling alley, and a big ass pool in the back. The shit was crazy.

Once I hit the landing, I heard a familiar voice that sent an instant electric charge through my chest.

"Cole know you dressed like that?" Quan's deep, rough voice came from the living room.

"Quan mind your business." Kenya laughed. "Blaze give me another shot."

I found my way to the room and my eyes landed on Blaze first, who walked towards me sporting a bad ass off the shoulder, skin tight, spandex dress. It was a cute little piece that stopped right at her calves. The clear, chunky heel, sandal stilettoes on her feet gave her little short ass some height. The messy bun on her head looked real cute, and her makeup was fire.

by *Nique Luarks*

"You want a shot?" She asked, stopping in front of me.

"Yeah, you got Patron?" My eyes shifted to Ava. For some reason I felt the need to avoid eye contact with DaQuan.

"We got Patron, Dusse, and tequila..." She turned around. "Ava, you said tequila, right?" She waited for Ava's clarification.

"Yeah." She snapped her fingers like she'd forgotten something. "I know Kai got some shells."

Blaze walked past me. "Yep, I'll be right back."

Ava danced playfully. "Damn, Keyshia, you don't be coming to play with these hoes." Ava switched towards me. "Three-sixty?"

I smirked, doing a slow spin so she could check me out.

"All my bitches bad," she boasted proudly.

"Ain't we?" Kenya agreed.

Both she and Ava looked like they belonged in a music video. They were both rocking Bodycons. The only difference was Kenya's was white and Ava's was red. Both were serving body, looking like money. Kenya's hair was in a long, silky ponytail and Ava was rocking her signature pixie cut. I nodded my head in approval. The night was sure to be one for the books.

These niggas are about to eat their hearts out.

COVERED IN YOUR LOVE 2
by *Nique Luarks*

"Where ya'll going?" Kai Money entered the room with his phone to his ear.

All three of us looked at each other.

"I'll accept an answer from either one of ya'll."

Kenya smacked her lips. "Nobody in here is named Blaze." Rolling her eyes, she went and sat down on the couch.

"Cole know you got that on?" He frowned.

"Nope," Quan's messy ass blurted out.

"Quan, don't you have a baby to go take care of?" Ava rolled her eyes.

"Don't you got a dick to go suck?" he shot back coolly.

Kai chuckled.

"What's funny?" She took a seat next to Kenya. "And don't worry about the dicks I suck."

Kenya laughed.

Blaze entered the room carrying a tray with shots on it. "Patron for Ry..." She stopped next to me.

I took two shots off the tray. "Thank you."

Ava hopped up. "Let me get my two so we can ride out. These niggas is fuckin' up my vibe." She took her shots off the tray.

"Blaze, where you going?" Kai asked.

"Out," she answered with her back to him. "And Dusse for my girl and me." She stopped in front of Kenya.

"Out where?" he pressed.

"Why? So ya'll can show up and run all the niggas away? No." Ava tossed her shots back.

"Fuck all that." Kai waved her off. "Where are you going?"

"We got a section at Glacier," she tattled.

Kenya huffed. "Well,there goes my night. I told ya'll we should've gotten a room and dressed there."

"That's Blaze's ole snitching ass," Ava pouted, sitting her glasses down on the end table.

"Cause Blaze got a husband," Kai said before leaving the room.

Quan stood up and made his way over to me. "You can't speak now?" Looking down on me, he licked those lips and I had flashbacks of the night we'd spent together just days ago.

"What's up?" I played it cool.

"You look pretty, My Ry." His eyes roamed over my ensemble.

"Thanks."

He rubbed his thumb softly across the tattoo behind my ear. "You smell good too."

"Thanks." I stared back at him.

"Taste even better." He smirked, and I almost choked on my spit.

"Y'all just nasty." Kenya snickered, walking past us and out the living room.

"Right, little freaks." Ava followed suit with a giggling Blaze right on her heels.

"You need something?" he asked, digging in his pockets for what I knew was cash.

"Nah, I'm straight." Declining his offer, I stepped around him and headed for the front door where my girls were waiting on me.

Jaime

After we'd gone and enjoyed some good food, Nas dropped Duke and me back off and went his separate way. Jaylen convinced me to bake a cake, so we were both in my kitchen sipping wine.

"You're really feeling him, huh?" She sat across from me at the kitchen island.

I smiled. "Yeah. We're just so damn dysfunctional."

I'd honestly thought Nas would stop messing with me when I got home from the hospital. When he left my room that day, we didn't speak unless he was calling to talk to Duke. Jade had tried to convince me it was weird for him to still want to have a relationship with my son and not me. Jaylen, on the other hand, was all for it. Like me, she agreed Duke needed a consistent male in his life, and surprisingly, Duke's behavior was changing drastically. He still had his moments when I had to threaten him with a belt, but for the most part, his attitude was getting better.

"What relationship ain't dysfunctional, though?" Jaylen reached for the bottle of wine. "It takes patience and understanding. Two things Nas seems to have with your stubborn ass." She snickered, refilling her glass.

She was right. Since I'd met Nas, I'd been giving him a hard time. Yet he still had managed to win me over. I wasn't in love, but I damn sure was in lust. Truth be told, when he called on Christmas, I'd already had plans on having a sit down with him and apologizing for my attitude.

My phone rang as I iced the cake with chocolate frosting, which was Duke's favorite. "That's him now." Answering the phone, I put it on speaker.

"Brother-in-law..." Jaylen spoke, giggling.

"What up, sis?" His deep voice made my kitty thump. "Where my baby at?"

Jaylen grinned at me.

"Right here. What's up?" I continued icing the cake.

"Bout to roll up and ride out wit' the fam," he told me and then told somebody to mind their business.

"Where ya'll going?"

"Out. You wanna come?"

I shook my head as if he could see me. "I don't have a babysitter."

"I'll babysit." Jaylen stood up. "He's sleep anyway. Jade asked if she could drop Shane off so I'll have a little sleep overwith her and Maxx."

Damn it, Jaylen.

***

"Nas is outside." Jaylen sat down on my bed next to me. "You look cute or whateva."

"Thanks," I said, sliding my feet into my red thigh-high boots. Looking at the clock on my night stand, I saw it was going on midnight.

"So, where are you going?" She combed through my hair with her fingers.

"I don't know. He didn't say." Once I had both boots on, I stood up.

"My lil' sister is fine." She grinned, smacking my bare thigh. "I see you got these thick thighs out. Slay, honey."

"I'm older than you." I frowned. "This ain't too short, is it?" I looked down at my tight, mesh black Bodycon dress. "You don't think it's too cold?"

The dress seemed like a good choice before I'd hopped in the shower, now I was second guessing it. I wasn't sure I was digging how short it was.

"Nope."

COVERED IN YOUR LOVE 2
by *Nique Luarks*

"You sure?" I made my way to my dresser to put my jewelry on.

"Yep."

"Jaylen, for real?" I was about to change my mind altogether. I could link up with Nas and his crew some other time.

"Meme, oh my God." She rolled her eyes, helping me put my Nas necklace one.

Sliding a set of gold rings onto my middle finger, I sighed nervously.

"You trippin'."

I picked up my gold, diamond earrings. "I wish you were going, so I would know *somebody*." Yeah, I was most definitely having doubts now.

"Somebody you know *is* going—*Nas*." She started pushing me out of my room.

"Wait. Let me switch out my purse." I chuckled, securing the back on my earring.

"Girl, you rolling wit' a baller tonight. You don't need no damn purse." She laughed, *still* pushing me out of my own room.

We made our way down the stairs with Jaylen fixing my hair, telling me I'd better have fun and stop worrying. That was me, though. I worried. I'd been through way too much in my life not to. Then after the type of day I'd had with my daddy and Jade, I really just wanted to lay across my bed and think and mediate.

Reaching the landing, I faced Len. "So, I look alright?" I did a quick spin. "How does my makeup look?"

"You look fine, Jaime. And your makeup perfect." She rolled her eyes. "That red lip goes perfectly with your boots." She pushed past me and opened the door. "Now, get out."

"How are you kicking me out of my own house?" I stood in the entrance.

"Bye, Jaime. I know what you're doing." She started to close the door on me. "Quit stalling. And ride his dick all night. Make Amber Rose proud." She snickered.

"Later, Len." I shook my head at my sister as she closed the door.

Nervously, I waltzed to Nas' red Lambo. Even though his windows were rolled up, I could hear 21 Savages' "Bank Account" blaring from inside. Getting my nerves and the butterflies in my stomach together, I opened the passenger's door. Sliding onto the plush, heated seat, I was hit with the whiff of weed. Closing my door, I fixed the bottom of my dress and faced Nas just as he turned the music down.

"What's up, baby?" He leaned in for a kiss and I gladly gave him a wet one. It was crazy how every time our lips locked it felt like the very first time. Like, my knees literally felt weak, and my heart was about to burst out of my chest. Then the way he stared at me when he pulled back made me want to say fuck the club, take Jaylen's advice, and hop right on his dick.

"Hey." I blushed unintentionally. That was the effect he had on me, though. Making me do things I usually didn't do, like being all open and shit.

"You look mad dope." He ran his fingers through my hair.

"Thank you."

He nodded.

"So where are we going?" I asked, pulling the seatbelt across my body.

"Out." He passed me a Styrofoam cup. "It's Remy." He put the luxury whip in drive and peeled off.

I nodded and he turned the music back up a little. "I feel overdressed." I couldn't see the shoes he had on, but the white and black Nike windbreaker he had wasn't club attire. The black NY fitted cap on his head was hiding his deep waves, but as usual, he was draped in gold and diamonds.

"I wasn't planning to go out. It's last minute." He shrugged, lighting a blunt. "Plus I'm gangster. so I wear what the fuck I want to the club. I ain't got nobody to impress but you." I then noticed the glock sitting on his lap. I'd almost missed it because of his black jeans.

"Okay." I took a long sip out of my cup.

"Plus…" He took a long drag of the weed. "My girl is sexy as a muthafucka." Exhaling through his nostrils, he passed it to me. "All I need to do is stand by her and we'll both look good."

I looked out the window and smiled

"I see you over there cheesing. I ain't speakin' nothin' but facts."

I chuckled before hitting the blunt.

"Was Duke still sleep when you left?" He stopped at a red light and faced me.

Blowing smoke from my mouth, I nodded.

"Cool." He sped off.

See, little things like checking in with my son drew me closer to him. Nas asked more about Duke than Troy did. Hell, Duke hadn't spoken to his daddy since Christmas. Nas was making it too easy for me to fall for him. He cared about Duke's safety and happiness the same way he did mine.

Passing the smoke back to him, I got comfortable in my seat and reached for his phone to pick a song. He was already on 21 Savages album, so I picked a song randomly since I'd bumped the whole album when it first came out. Turning the volume back up, I sat back in my seat as we coasted through traffic. I took a sip from my cup the same time he handed me the blunt again. Nas gripped my thigh as I took a long toke.

Jaylen was right. What did I have to be worried about? I knew Nas would make sure I was good no matter what. Duke was safe at home in his bed and unlike Jade, Jaylen was a responsible adult. The weed and liquor was kicking and I was riding shotgun in a fuckin' Lamborghini. What's the worst that could happen?

Chapter Eleven

Loyalty

Quan

I pulled up to the club right behind Kai and Cole. Blaze and Kenya should've known better than to think them niggas was letting them out without the team. We didn't club much, but whenever we did, we came as a unit. Kai Money didn't play that shit about his wife. As soon as the ladies left, Nana Haley put the twins to bed. Twenty minutes after that, Cole was dropping CJ off with her too.

Hopping out my whip, I tucked my burner in my jeans and shut my door. Since none of us had planned to come out, I was dressed in a grey Gucci tracksuit and wheat Timbs. Fixing the chains around my neck, I made my way over to Cole's Wraith.

"Heeeey, Quan," a voice said, but I kept on walking. There was only one chick I was checking for. I made it to Cole's ride the same time Kai did, lighting a L.

"Where Nas?" Cole shut his door.

"Shit, I don't know." I shrugged, running my hand across the top of my head. "Said he was pulling up, though."

126

Kai nodded.

"So, you tryna get Ry's ass back, huh?" Cole smirked knowingly. He was probably the only person who knew I'd cried real-life tears behind Ryan.

"She ain't fuckin' wit me like that." I looked around at our surroundings.

"Dom and them are already here in there." Kai started leading the way to the entrance.

"It's brick as fuck out here, yo." After rubbing my hands together, I then stuffed them in the front of my sweats slightly.

"Kai!" We pushed through the crowd. "Kai! Can I roll with ya'll?" Shorty in a black cat suit, standing in the long-ass line called out.

Once we reached the entrance, the bouncer made room for us to get by. "Look who's in the muthafuckin' building!" We dapped him up one by one. "The ladies got a section at the top," he informed us.

The joint was packed for a Wednesday night, but I knew our boys were in the spot heavy in case some shit jumped off. Bitches were half naked, of course and niggas were posted up against the wall checking out the scenery.

"Oh Shit! The Fam is the building!" The deejay shouted over the music into a mic. "What's up, Kai Money? What it do, Cole? I see you, Quan! Nas, what's good?

Chucking up my set, I turned around to see Nas coming through the door with his lil' chick, Jaime. I could see why he was on her heels, though. Baby was bad. Nas pulled her in front of him and whispered in her ear. Continuing our route to the VIP area, I ignored a couple of bitches that were damn near throwing themselves into my arms.

We reached the VIP and just like I knew they would be, the ladies were already on one. When we stepped into their section, Cardi B was blasting, rapping about making money moves. Ava and Kenya looked to be the ringleaders, looking over the balcony holding bottles of Cîroc, rapping the lyrics loud. Blaze was recording and Ryan was sitting on the couch, lost in her phone.

Who the fuck she texting?

Probably that nigga she was fuckin' in Missouri.

I grimaced just thinking about the shit. Making my way over to her, I sat down and snatched her phone out of her hand.

"Um...can you give me my shit back?" She tried to snatch it back.

by *Nique Luarks*

I noticed she was on her Snapchat. "Who you over here Snapchatting?"

"That ain't none of your business. Give me my phone back." I moved my hand away when she attempted to snatch it out of my hands again.

"You are my business." I frowned.

"Since when?" She chuckled, taking a sip from her cup.

"Since forever." I scooted closer.

"DaQuan," she huffed. "Like...come on, yo." She tucked a piece of her silky hair behind her ear.

"So, I can't even talk to you?" I handed her phone back to her.

"I didn't say that."

She was acting like I hadn't just been breaking her fuckin' back in. I knew sex wouldn't fix or change nothing between us, but I at least wanted us to be cordial. Even if Ry didn't want to be with a nigga, I still wanted her in my life. So, her business would forever be mine. *She* would forever be my muthafuckin nigga.

"Then what are you saying?" I pressed.

"I'm *saying* mind your business." She snickered because she knew she'd gotten under my skin.

by *Nique Luarks*

I chuckled. "A'ight."

"You excited about the new edition?" She took a gulp of the clear liquid in her cup.

"Why you doing that, man?" I sighed, leaning further back into my seat. Immediately, I felt like shit.

"You know what?" She stood up. "I'll see you later." I watched her walk away and go stand at the balcony by Ava. Kenya was now sitting in Cole's lap laughing. Looking around at my boys with their women made me feel and look just like a straight chump. Even Nas seemed to be caking with his shorty.

Leaning forward, I picked up a bottle of Patron out of the ice bucket and popped the seal. I would do anything to have Ry blowing up my phone, getting on my damn nerves like she used to. She wasn't stunting me now and the shit was fuckin' with my pride *and* ego. I'd fucked up royally and there was a great chance we would never bounce back from this shit. Drinking out of the bottle, I shook my head in disappointment.

"Why are you over here pouting?" Ava plopped down next to me.

"I'm chillin'," I spoke, but stared at Ry as she switched her way over to Nas. Why the fuck did she have to be so flyy? And then she had the nerve to do the shit effortlessly.

"Nigga, please. You stalking the fuck out of Ryan."

I sipped from the bottle.

"Creep ass." She sniggled.

"What you want?" Finally, I faced her.

"I can't chill with my brother?" She grinned.

"I don't wanna chill wit' you. Didn't you come out to celebrate for Ry?" I wanted to shoo her instigating ass away.

She held her chest. "Damn, it's like that?" She laughed. "And I did come to kick it wit' my girls. That's why I'm trying to figure out why Nas brought that Jaime chick. She ain't family."

"Yo, Ava, you better stop while you ahead." Nas don't play when it came to shorty. I witnessed him curse his own sister, Nikki, the fuck out behind Jaime.

She waved me off. "That bitch don't want no smoke with me."

"Why you trippin'?" I side eyed her. "Let me find out."

"Find out what?" She sucked her teeth. "She came in our section and didn't even speak," she argued.

"Then shut up and go fuckin' speak."

"That's not how this works."

I only stared at her. I don't know why Ava thought she was queen bitch. Maybe it was because she hung with us, but the shit was getting out of control. Her little spoiled ass was starting to get on everybody's nerves. If she had beef with Jaime, then she was going to have to get over it and nip that dumb shit in the bud. Clearly, shorty was family now.

Suddenly, all the ladies stood up simultaneously, including Jaime, and headed towards the exit.

"Ava, we're going to the dance floor!" Kenya's loud ass hollered.

Ryan, who looked to be good and drunk now, was laughing, saying something to Blaze.

Jaime seemed to be in her own zone, but she fit right into their little clique, sipping out of her cup, swaying to the music.

Ava hopped up. "Aye!"

One by one, they left out of the VIP, talking and laughing loud.

Jaime

Blaze, Kenya, and Ryan were cool as hell. When I first stepped into the VIP and saw how pretty and flyy everybody was I figured they were stuck up. Boy was I wrong. Blaze was quiet, kind of like me, but she was so down to earth. She giggled a lot at Kenya, who was a party all by herself. She was short like me, but her presence held a lot of power.

Kenya so far seemed to be one big ball of fun and laughs. Like Blaze, she was gorgeous, but they were like night and day. From their skin complexion to their height, but I almost instantly picked up on their vibe and noticed they were best friends. Ryan didn't say much, but she was the first one to come over and introduce herself to me. She was just as bright as Kenya, covered in tattoos, with a small beauty mark right above her lip. One look at Ryan and you knew she'd beat a bitch's ass, but she was beautiful.

The only one who hadn't said one word to be was Ava; not that I was surprised. I'd met her at the block party not too long ago and sensed she wasn't really feeling me. Tonight was no different, because every time she looked at me she rolled her eyes. Ava was stunning with the same soft chocolate complexion as me, a dope pixie cut, and a Marilynn Monroe piercing. Like Ryan, I got the impression she was about that life.

As long as she kept it cordial with me, I would do the same. But I hoped she didn't get too liquored up and try me. I was small, but I didn't play that shit. She could mean mug all she wanted, but the moment she said some slick shit to me, I was more than willing to put her pretty ass in check. We were all headed to the dance floor to get away from the men, and all I wanted to do was have a good time.

"Migos-Motorsport" was bumping through the club as we rushed to dance floor. For it to be a weekday, the club was lit. Blaze grabbed my hands and started dancing, making me laugh at how goofy she was. Kenya egged her on when she started twerking. Ryan was rapping Nicki Minaj's part.

"You bitches catchin' a fade, shout out my nigga Lil Boosie
All of your friends'll be dead, you can get hit with that Uzi
I call him Ricky, he say he love me like Lucy
Get you a straw nigga, you know this pussy is juicy"
Ava grabbed a random dude and started dancing on him.

I was actually having a good time. I hadn't laughed and danced this much in a long time.

"Uhh Meme!" I stopped dancing when I heard what sounded like Jade.

Turning around, I faced my sister who had a mean scowl on her face. "Jay! Hey!" I grinned. The alcohol and weed I'd consumed had done its job.

"Who are *they*?" She put her hands on her hips. Her whole vibe threw me off.

"Blaze!" Blaze stopped dancing. "We're family." She smiled

Kenya stopped moving too and so did Ryan. Ava, however, had made her way to the bar with the dude she'd been grinding on.

"This is my little sister and I've never seen her wit' ya'll before," Jade sassed. Her nose was turned up and everything.

"Is that a reason for you to have an attitude, though?" Kenya frowned.

"Right," Ryan cosigned.

"Ken...Ry..." Blaze started.

Jade, not tonight…

I sighed, visibly irritated. Blaze and the girls were cool and all, but if some shit popped off I was most definitely team Jade. I wasn't sure why she had an attitude, but I needed to get her alone to find out. The look on Kenya's face let me know she

135

wasn't for the bullshit and Ryan's whole demeanor had changed. They were ready for a fight.

"Let's go back to the VIP."

Thank you, Blaze.

I took note to how she was still smiling, gently pulling Kenya by her arm.

"I'll meet ya'll up there." I said, still looking at Jade, who rolled her eyes at Ryan as she walked by. Pulling her towards the bar, we stood a few feet away from Ava and her friend.

"For somebody who don't like clubbing, you sho' out here kicking it with these random-ass bitches."

"Nas invited me out," I explained even though I didn't have to. Like Blaze, I just wanted to keep the peace.

"So, you couldn't invite me?" She mugged me. "That's fucked up. You know me and my girls like to party."

"I was *invited*, Jade, which means I was *asked* by someone else. Why would I invite you somewhere I was invited to?" She was beginning to piss me off.

"Because I'm your sister and you don't know these bitches like that."

"Excuse you?" Ava came from nowhere and jumped in our conversation.

"I'm talking to my sister." Jade waved her off.

"Yeah...a'ight." Ava smirked, walking away. "Bum-ass bitch," she threw over her shoulder.

I grabbed Jade by her forearm before she could walk towards her. "Why are you trippin'?"

"I'm straight," she slurred, and right then and there I knew she was drunk.

"Who are you here with?"

"Myeisha and them." She looked around. "Look, I'm bout to find my home girls. Go live it up with the mafia." She rolled her eyes and stormed away.

I watched her walk towards the bathroom, shaking my head. As I made my way through the crowd, I noticed Nas heading right for me. Everybody made a walkway for him to get through and I chuckled inwardly. They were probably trying to make sure they didn't step on the white Timbs on his feet. His ass was so intimidating.

"You good?" He pulled me to his chest.

"Yeah, I had to talk to Jade."

He nodded. "Come on."

I led the way back to the section with his hand on the small of my back. I wasn't going to let Jade ruin my night. When we entered the section it was somewhat packed. Men I recognized Nas shooting dice with the first time I'd met him were in attendance and half-naked woman were smiling in their faces. Leaving Nas' side, I went to take a seat with the ladies.

"Everything okay?" Blaze asked as I took a seat next to her.

"Yeah, that's Jade." I shrugged. "Sorry about that."

Ryan nodded.

"She's on one. She better slow her ass down before she run across the right one." Kenya laughed, handing me a cup.

I chuckled. "She'll be a'ight."

The party picked back up full swing and the men started shooting dice. I noticed Ava was the only woman in their circle. Nas said she was like a sister, so I figured she'd probably always been that way. Not too long after I'd finished my third cup, I stood up and made my way over to Nas. He was looking down at the dice game with a serious, sexy expression on his face.

"Hey." I wrapped my arms around his torso.

He looked down at me. "What's up, baby? You straight?" He kissed my forehead.

"Yeah." I gazed up at him lustfully. Nas was such an alpha male.

"Get yo lovey-dovey ass out the D-game," Cole joked just as Kenya came to his side.

"Shut up." She bumped him playfully, and he pulled her close.

Nas kissed my neck.

"Ugh."

I looked to Ava just as she rolled her eyes. "Ugh what?" left my lips before I could stop it. All night she'd been getting on my nerves.

"Was I talking to you?" Her hands moved as she held a bottle of Dusse in her right hand.

"No, but you were talking about me." I let go of Nas. "You got a problem wit' me?"

"Nas, you better get ya girl." She chuckled, eyeing me evilly.

"Ah shit," Quan mumbled, shaking his head.

"No, he needs to get *your* ass. You're the one wit' the fuckin' issue." I frowned.

The crazy bitch threw the bottle of Dusse at me and it hit me on my shoulder hard. It would've hit my face if I hadn't tried to dodge it. Almost immediately, the entire section went into an uproar as I tried to get to her and she tried to get to me.

"Bitch!" I screamed as Nas held onto my waist.

"Let her go, Nas! I'm tired of this bitch's mouth!" she hollered as Quan bear hugged her.

"Baby, chill," Nas whispered in my ear. "I'ma handle it."

Tears built in my eyes. This bitch really had me fucked up. Nas did too if he thought she was about to get that shit off. I struggled to get out of his grasp, but he had a tight hold on me, which further infuriated me.

"Ava, take your ass on!" Kai hollered.

"What?!" she screamed. "Are you for real?! She started with me!"

"Ava, I'ma get wit' you later," he dismissed her.

" I'm ready to go," I spoke. "Let me go, Nasir," I demanded, tugging away from him, only because he let me.

"A'ight." He sighed. "Man, we out."

Ava crossed her arms over her chest, smirking as we started out of the area. I swear my blood started boiling the closer we got to her. Nas was saying something to me, but I wasn't trying to hear shit he had to say. The music picked back up and the party kept on going. Ava was now only a few steps away from me, dancing like she hadn't just thrown a fuckin' bottle at my face.

I'ma kill this bitch.

Nas held on to me as we walked past the table filled with alcohol and in a swift, quick motion, I snatched up a bottle of French Vanilla Cîroc. His hold had loosened, so I was able to yank away from his grasp. Charging towards Ava, I hit her ass over the head. Bet the bitch won't throw nothing else.

Chapter Twelve

...A drastic turn of events

Nas

"Daaaaamn!" somebody yelled as I snatched Jaime's little violent ass up.

"Oooooh!"

Ava hit the floor. Blaze rushed to her aide and tried to help her up.

"I wish you would throw another bottle at me, hoe!" Jaime screamed, trying to get loose. "Let me go!" She continued to try to wiggle free.

"Baby, man…" I was growing frustrated. I didn't bring Jaime out for her to be fighting and shit. I told her I would handle Ava's ass.

"Fuck all that!" she continued yelling at the top of her fuckin' lungs.

Finally, having enough, I picked her up and tossed her over my shoulder. Holding down the back of her dress with my free hand, I left out the VIP. For Jaime to be so small, she was strong as hell. She made it hard for me to get her down the stairs and to the exit. By the time we reached the bottom of the steps, she was damn near fighting *me*.

Putting her down, I yoked her little feisty ass up by her shoulders. "Calm yo ass the fuck down!" I hollered in her face.

"Fuck you!" she yelled back.

I'ma whoop her ass.

Yanking her by her arm, I pulled her towards the door.

"Ouu!"She whimpered, making me realize I'd probably been to rough.

Letting her go, I picked her up honeymoon style. "I'm sorry." I kissed her face. "Did I hurt you?"

"Put me down." Tears lined the brim of her eyes, making me feel like shit.

"Meme!" Jade ran up on me. "What the fuck did you do my sister?" She yelled trying to tug Jaime out of my arms.

"Bitch, move!" I palmed her forehead and roughly pushed her dumb ass back. Her drunk ass stumbled trying to catch her balance.

"Nas! So, it's like that?" It seemed like Myeisha came from nowhere.

Putting Jaime down, I held onto her waist. "Eisha, take yo simple ass on somewhere. You and this hoe got me fucked up." These bitches must've forgotten who the fuck I was.

"I been calling, nigga," she popped off.

"So?" Jaime chimed in.

"Meme, stay out of it," Jade snapped.

"Shut the fuck up, Jade!" Jaime jumped in her face.

"Nas,we good?" The bouncer came up on me.

"Yeah, I'm straight." I waved him off.

"A'ight." He nodded then walked away. He was on Kai's payroll so he knew to turn a blind eye to anything pertaining us until told otherwise.

"Meme, this nigga got you trippin'." Jade rolled her long-ass neck. "Whole time he fuckin' Eisha and the whole hood is laughing at you."

"Facts," Myeisha cosigned. "

"Bitch, quit lyin'." I hadn't fucked with Eisha like that in weeks. I hoped Jaime didn't believe that bullshit.

"Jay, what the fuck is wrong with you!?" Jaime hopped in her face. "Bitch, I'm your *sister*! Your loyalty lies with me."

"Jaime, you better get the fuck out my face before I drop your ass." Jade stepped in her face. "Myeisha been realer than your wanna-be-Ms. Perfect ass has." She smirked and I could've sworn I saw my baby's shoulders drop.

Myeisha snickered.

"Go find somebody's husband to fuck and suck on."

"Oh shit!" the rest of Myeisha's crew cosigned, standing behind them.

Jaime's tiny ass was on a mission, because she snatched Jade by her hair and yanked her down to the ground. Jaime started fuckin' her up, which was why Eisha thought she was hopping in. I rocked her shit, hitting her dead in her mouth, sending her flying back into her home girls.

"Uh uh, Nas!" Cameron yelled. "That's fucked up." She held on to a dazed Eisha.

Ignoring her, I tried to pull Jaime off of her sister. She wasn't having it, though.

"Bitch…" She punched Jade in the face. "You got all…" She kicked her. "That fuckin' mouth!" She yanked her by her head and started dragging her.

"What the hell!" Ryan rushed down the stairs. "Bro, what the fuck is going on?" she addressed me.

"Uh uh, bitch, ain't no jumpin'!" Cameron pushed Ry back.

She done fucked up.

COVERED IN YOUR LOVE 2
by *Nique Luarks*

Ry cocked her fist back and slugged the shit out of Cameron. Eisha's crew somehow doubled and bitches tried to jump on Ryan and Jaime. I was tossing bitches and pulling them apart when I heard what sounded like Kenya saying, *"Oh hell nah!"* The shit turned into a full-throttle brawl when she and Blaze hopped in the mix, banging like a muthafucka. Finally, when I was able to pull Jaime off of Jade, I bear hugged her to keep her from fuckin' me up too.

"Baby!" I hollered. Kissing her neck, I tried to calm her down. "Relax, baby. Chill out, man." I started to pull her away from the commotion.

Tat, Tat, Tat, Tat, Tat.

A tech nine went off and the club went into frenzy. Immediately, I went for my glock. That's when I noticed Kai Money was the one who let the shots off. He had a pissed-off look on his face as everybody scurried around him.

He picked an enraged Blaze up and headed for the back of the club. Cole rushed after him carrying Kenya. Quan followed right behind damn near dragging Ryan's gangster ass. I tossed Jaime back over my shoulder, speed walking out of the back door.

Ryan

The cold air hit my face, calming me down a little. My adrenaline was still pumping, though as Quan pulled me towards a black Phantom. I hadn't planned on fighting, but when I was coming down the stairs from the VIP and saw Nas trying to pull Jaime off of her sister, I knew some shit was about to go down. Quan opened the back door and I got in with him right behind me. The driver was already sitting behind the steering wheel, and after the okay from Quan, he peeled out of the parking lot.

We rode in silence until his phone started going off. He quickly looked down at the screen and pressed ignore, letting me know exactly who it was calling. Instantly, I got pissed. I don't know what came over me, but I slid my left foot out of my boot and gripped it tight. His phone went off again and I lost it.

Whap! Whap!

I smacked him right across the face with the heel of my boot.

Whap!

I started crying.

Whap!

We wrestled as he tried to stop me from hitting him again. I could literally feel the car rocking as we tussled, but the driver continued coasting through traffic. I yanked the collar of the white T-shirt underneath his Gucci hoodie, ripping it instantly. Balling my fist up, I tried to send a blow to his nose, but his quick ass blocked it. Finally, he was able to get a decent hold on me and rested his heavy body on top of mine.

"Ry!" He pinned me back awkwardly against the seat and door.

"Get off me!" I screamed.

"What the fuck, yo?!" he yelled in my face. "What the fuck is wrong wit you?!" The puzzled look on his sexy face made me want to strike him with my shoe again.

"Get the fuck off of me!" I broke down crying. "I hate yo dumb ass." I bawled. "I hope you die."

His face dropped and he hung his head.

I didn't really mean it, but the way my broken heart was set up, I'd say anything. Anything for him to feel the same kind of hurt I was feeling at this very moment. Quan was having a baby, and even though I'd tried to act like I wasn't bothered by it, the shit was killing me slowly. How could he do this to me...to *us*?

I cried.

"Ry, stop, yo." He pressed his lips against my neck. "Stop crying."

"You and that bitch belong together." I moved my face when he tried to kiss my lips.

"No, we don't. I belong wit' you," he tried to convince me.

I sniffled as he tongue kissed my neck. "Stop, Quan." He let go of my arms and I pushed him hard in the chest.

"I'm sorry, Ryan," he mumbled, pulling down on the waistband of my jeans.

"Move!"

He yanked my pants and panties clean off my left leg in one swift motion. Grabbing my ankle, he slid me across the seat until I was lying flat on my back. When his phone went off again, I tried to wiggle out of his grasp. I was almost free when I felt the head of his bare dick sliding into my pussy. Unconsciously, I opened my legs wider and allowed him full access to my love.

"Mmmm…" His mouth covered mine.

"I love you, baby," he moaned. "I love you so much, Ry. Don't leave me." His deep voice was raspy as he begged. "I can fix it."

No, you can't.

I closed my eyes enjoying how good he felt. How could we move forward? It was impossible for me to be second in his life. Since I'd known him, I had always been his number one priority.

A baby would change that. He couldn't fix this. The damage was done.

"Ssshit." I wrapped my arms around his neck.

Pushing my legs back, he fucked me harder. Stretching me out, he wrapped one hand around my neck and tongued me down. I was so turned on I kissed him back hungrily, savoring the moment. He continued pounding down on my spot, damn near fucking me off the seat. A tingling sensation traveled from my toes to the top of my head and I knew exactly what was about to happen next.

"Aaaaagggh!" I screamed as a body-rocking, soul-shifting, breath-taking orgasm shot through my body and right onto the leather seat.

"Fuck," he groaned, but wouldn't let up; not even when my entire body started jerking.

My eyes rolled to the back of my head and everything went still as I rode the wave.

"Fuuuccck!" Quan's body froze and the only thing that kept on moving was his dick as it jerked violently, filling me up.

Chapter Thirteen

Love bound

Jaime

"Mama!"

The sound of Duke's voice woke me up. Squinting my eyes, I pulled the cover up over my naked body. "Hey Bean."

"You sleep?" he asked, leaning on his elbows directly in front of me.

"Nope." I covered my mouth to yawn. Reaching for my iPhone on Nas' nightstand, I checked the time.

"Yo, Duke..." Nas entered the room in nothing but basketball shorts. "Go eat, dude."

"Okay." Duke took off running out of the room.

"You went and picked up Duke?" I sat up.

"Yeah." Sitting down on the bed with his back to me, he leaned forward on his elbows. "Jaylen was blowing your phone up and shit."

Scrolling through my phone, I saw Jaylen had indeed called me numerous times and sent a total of twenty-three text messages. Already knowing what the conversation was going to be about, I opted out of reaching back. Scooting backwards until my back was against his head board, I shook my head at last night's shenanigans. I'd let Ava and Jade bring me out of character. That hoe, Ava, was a non-factor, but I wasn't through with Jade.

"She asked you to come and get him?" I'm sure Jade had spoken to Jaylen, but I didn't know if she had chosen a side or not. We were both wrong. No matter what, we were family and we could've handled each other way better than that. I knew my mother was disappointed in us but more so, in me, because I'd always been the glue to hold our sisterhood together.

"Nah, Duke was looking for you. She did say hit her up, though." His tatted back was still to me. If I wasn't tripping, he sounded like he had an attitude.

"Okay." The room fell into an awkward silence.

I watched as he ran his hand across his head. The big bold letters across the top of his back read *Family First*. Jade crossed my mind again. I wondered what Nas thought about what she said. I'm sure he'd heard her loud and clear. Maybe that's why he was acting like I was bothering him.

Turning sideways, he stared at me. His mouth didn't move, but the look in his eyes spoke volumes.

He's mad at me.

Fidgeting with the pillow in my hand, I broke my eyes away from his cold ones.

"How many niggas you fuckin'?" His stare hardened.

"What?" I was truly confused. Where was all this coming from?

"Keep playin' wit me, Jaime." He stood up.

"I don't know what the fuck you're talking about?" I snapped, holding on to the comforter tighter.

Stalking over to my side, he leaned over me menacingly. "You still fuckin' your baby daddy?"

Is he for real right now?

Tossing the covers off of my body, I pushed him back hard in the chest. I caught an instant attitude when he didn't budge. Why the hell was he so built? I attempted to get past him, but he grabbed my forearm, stopping me. In my nakedness, I glared back at him.

"Nas, let go of me." Yanking my arm away, I tried to side step him.

He blocked me. "Answer my fuckin' question."

"Nas, you're sitting here disrespecting me. Take us home."

"Why the fuck that nigga blowing your phone up? He's texting you all day and shit!" he growled. "You tryna get that nigga murdered?"

"Do you hear yourself! He's Duke's dad!"

"So, he didn't text you asking if he could spend the night?"

My heart dropped to me feet, because he did. I never responded

back because that's what Troy does. Even though he knows I'll
never mess with him like that again, he still tries his hand. In his
fucked up mind he thinks he still actually has a chance with me.
I'd told him time and time again he would never have me in that
way again. If he'd put that much effort into trying to build a
relationship with his son, life could be so much easier.

"You went through my phone?" I frowned.

"The muthafuckin' been ringing since we got home!" he yelled
in my face. "When was the last time you fucked that bitch-ass
nigga?" His nose flared.

"None of your fuckin' business!" I yelled back. I could've easily
told him I hadn't touch Troy in a long time, but I didn't like
how he'd come at me. Nas was so used to bullying people, that
he was trying to use those same tactics in our relationship, but I
wasn't having it.

"Mama..." Duke stood at the threshold.

"Go put your shoes on, Bean," I spoke but continued staring at
Nas.

He stayed in the doorway.

"Duke, go downstairs for a minute." Nas looked over at him.

Slowly, he backed away from the door.

I'ma whoop his ass.

I didn't understand why he listened to Nas and not me. I was his
mother. I'd carried him for eight and a half months, breast fed
his greedy butt, and changed his shitty diapers. He'd known Nas
for thirty damn seconds and did whatever he was told. Could I
get some respect from *anyone?*

I was pissed.

"Quit telling my son what to do."

He waved me off. "Call that nigga right now."

"Who?" I tried to get past him again and he blocked me *again*.

"Yo baby daddy. Call that nigga, cause his ass bout to learn some fuckin' boundaries." He snarled.

"One, I'm not calling him and two, you're tripping." I crossed my arms over my bare chest.

Right on cue my phone went off in my hand. Nas quickly snatched it away from me before I could even see who was calling. Answering my phone, he took a step back. Grabbing his crotch, he eyed me as he answered the phone.

"What?" I'm not sure what the caller said, but the agitated look on his face was enough to let me know they'd said the wrong thing.

"Nas, give me my phone."

"Bitch, don't call this phone no more. Matter of fact, you gettin' that ass beat today. I'm tired of playing wit' yo hoe ass." He hung up.

"Nas!" He was really buggin'. "Give me my phone."

"You still fuckin' him?!" He jumped back in my face.

"No!" I was so mad that tears began to form in my eyes. "You see I didn't even respond to the messages."

"I don't want no more conversation wit' you and that nigga." He tossed my phone coolly onto the bed. Like he hadn't just been yelling at the top of his damn lungs.

"How will he talk to his son?" Nas was being overly dramatic. I couldn't believe he was acting like this.

"We're going to Sprint today. He needs his own phone anyway."

***

And that's how we wound up at the Sprint store, three hours and a shower make-up session later. Jaylen had sent a change of clothes for me so I hadn't even been home yet. I'd even turned my phone off and left it at Nas' house. After seeing it was Jade who'd called when Nas answered, I'd decided I was good on all bullshit for the day. Duke zoomed past me.

"Duke Warren." I raised an eyebrow. "What did I say about running indoors?" I pointed to a vacant seat. "Sit your ass down."

"Aw, he's too cute." The chick at the counter cooed to Nas as he walked toward her.

"Yeah, that's my dude. He needs a new phone."

"What kind of phone would you like to buy?" She leaned on her elbows, gazing up at Nas.

I chuckled.

"Give me the iPhone 8." He went into his pockets.

"The plus?" She stood up straight.

"Nah."

"Okay, you want to add the phone to your bill, right?" She started typing on her computer.

He nodded.

"Mama..." Duke jumped out of his seat and stood in front of me.

"Yeah, Bean?" I rubbed my hand across his fresh cut.

"I want some McDonald's." He leaned in closer to me. "I want some nuggets."

Kissing his forehead, I smiled at my baby. "I thought you wanted pizza?" On the short ride to the Sprint store he'd convinced Nas to buy pizza later.

"I do." He laughed. "I want pizza *and* nuggets." Wrapping his tiny arms around my neck, he put his nose on mine. "Why can't I have both?" His little silly butt grinned.

"Because that's not healthy. You don't need McDonald's."

"I need McDonald's." He stepped back abruptly. "Look." He then flexed with a serious expression on his face. "McDonald's gives me muscles." He giggled. "Touch my muscles, Mama."

I laughed slightly, squeezing down his on his little arms. "I see you."

"Baby, come here," Nas called out for me.

Standing up, I grabbed my purse. Duke slid his hands into mine as we approached the counter. "Yeah?"

"You wanna set his shit up for him in here or in the whip?" He stared down at me. "The service and shit is on."

I nodded. "Yeah, I can do it in the car."

The chick behind the counter sucked her teeth loudly.

Nas looked back at her. "Something wrong wit' yo fuckin' lips?"

Her eyes widened. "I-uhh..."

"Uhh uhh, my ass. You smackin' them big-ass lips like you wanna address an issue. What's up?"

"Nothing." She rolled her eyes. "Can I help you with something else?"

"Baby." Rubbing his arm, I pulled him away from the counter. We were going to have to work on his attitude.

He shook his head taking the bag off the counter, and then led the way to the door. Opening the door for me and Duke to get by, he slapped me hard on the ass.

Once we were all seated in the car comfortably with our seatbelts on, I took Duke's phone out of the box. As I busied myself with that, Nas whipped through traffic, talking on his phone. When he hung up, he looked over at me.

"We bout to go to my ole girl's house." He switched lanes.

"Your mother's house?" I stopped what I was doing.

"Yeah. She wanna meet you and Duke." His phone went off again.

I rolled my eyes. "Do you put that damn thing down?"

He chuckled. "For what? Money stay callin' a nigga. I gotta get to it."

Turning in my seat, I handed Duke his phone. "So, what's your mom like?" I watched Duke for a second before I faced forward again.

Nas shrugged lazily. "She a rider."

I smiled.

"You remind me a lot of her."

"How so?" I was intrigued.

"She's selfless."

"How do you know I'm selfless?" I grinned. "It took you forever to get a smile out of me." I waited with anxious eyes for his answer.

He chuckled. "That's another thing ya'll got in common."

"What?"

"Ya'll speak out of turn."

I slapped his arm playfully. "Really?"

"Yeah, man, you rude as fuck." He shook his head.

"Boy, you got your nerve." I snickered.

"See, we both know ain't shit about me boyish." He grinned exposing those pretty, straight, white teeth.

Butterflies. They made me feel somewhat queasy. I'd never felt this way around a man or *about* a man. I could get lost in Nas for hours. And that was just when I was thinking about him.

"Nah, but for real." He stopped at a stop sign and looked over at me. "I see you, Jaime." He licked his lips. "You shine bright as fuck, baby."

I blushed. "Thank you."

"For what?" He stared at me intently.

"The compliment," I mumbled bashfully. I felt like his eyes were burning a hole through my clothes. Like he was looking right into my soul, seeing something I didn't know was there.

Putting his truck in park, He put his right arm behind my headrest and gripped my chin. Making me look at him, he leaned forward and planted a soft kiss on my lips. When he pulled away, and I opened my eyes, he was directly in my face. Caressing my cheek, he stared at me long and hard. Unable to take his intensity, I shied away.

"What?" I whispered.

"You ain't ever gotta thank me for shit, Jaime. When I'm talking to you, I'm not just kicking shit to fill your head up. Any and everything I say to you won't be nothing but the real. And on some real shit, I should be thanking you."

Jesus.

"So, when I say you shine bright, you don't shy away from that shit like you don't already know it. You hear me?"

I nodded.

A horn went off, startling me. I'd completely forgotten we were sitting at a stop sign. Nas let me go and I looked out of my side mirror. Cars were lined up behind us waiting on us to move. Nas put the truck back in drive.

He sighed. "You trouble, man." Creases formed on his forehead as he went into deep thought.

You too…

Nas

Pulling into my mother's driveway, I shifted the gears and turned my truck off. Jaime and I really didn't say much after our conversation at the stop sign. Being around Jaime brought out feelings I wasn't used to. My lil' baby not knowing her worth was fucking with me. She looked in the mirror every day, so how could she not see what I saw?

Taking the keys out of the ignition, I opened my door. Stepping out, I placed my burner on my waist band and fixed my jeans. After shutting my door, I opened Duke's. Helping him out, I adjusted his Nike hoodie. I shut his door at the same time my sister, Nikki, pulled into the driveway behind me.

Not even waiting for her to get out of her ride, I went to Jaime's side. "You straight?"

"Yeah. I'm nervous, though." She put her hand in mine. "Duke, stop running in the grass."

"Leave that man alone."

"He just got those shoes." She pouted.

"And he can get some more." I placed her in front of me so she could climb the steps.

"Nas…" she started.

162

"Jaime…" I finished and she smacked her lips. "You smackin' them big-ass lips you like you wanna address an issue," I joked, making fun of the chick at the Sprint store.

She laughed, rolling her eyes at me.

I opened the door. "Ma!" Looking back into the yard, I called for Duke. "C'mon, lil' homie." I watched as he rushed towards the house.

"I'm hungry, Nas."

"When ain't you?" I chuckled, shaking my head at him as he ran past us. I was shocked Duke was as small as he was. His little ass could eat.

"Don't do my baby," Jaime sassed following me into the living room.

Jaime

"Nasir, whose baby is this running through my house?" a beautiful, slim woman with the same complexion as Nasir asked. She was dressed to kill in a tight black pencil skirt, a white silk button up, and spiked red bottoms. Her hair was pulled up into a messy bun, and she wore no makeup.

This can't be his mom.

"Ma, that's my guy," Nas confirmed what I refused to be the truth.

She looked way too young to have kids Nas' age. As a matter of fact, the only features that might've given her age away were the small creases on the corners of her brown, almond-shaped eyes. Her swag screamed thirty-six at the latest, not *forty-six*, which was how old Nas had said she was. She held her hand out smiling at me.

"You must be the infamous Jaime. I'm Noelle," she offered her name.

I smiled back, taking her manicured hand into mine. "It's nice to finally meet you."

"Same here. Oh, Nas, she's beautiful. You got your hands full with this one." She winked at me before turning on her heels.

"Where are ya'll coming from?" We followed behind her as her heels clicked loudly against the marble floors.

"Sprint," Nas answered.

"Duke!" I called out when I didn't hear my baby anymore.

"Huh?" We rounded the corner to find him sitting at the table digging in the grapes.

Embarrassed, I rushed towards him. "Really, Duke?" I lifted him up from the table and planted him on his feet. "I can't take you nowhere."

"He hungry." Nas of course came to his rescue.

"Oh, he's fine." Noelle chuckled. "Baby, you can have whatever you want," she spoke to Duke, taking a seat at the head of the table.

"Can I have this chicken?" He sat in the chair closest to her already holding a chicken leg.

I grimaced.

When the hell did he get that?

Noelle laughed. "Sure. "

Nas took the chair across from Duke and I took the seat to the left of Nas.

"How old are you, Duke?" Noelle asked him, fixing him a plate.

"Three." He chumped down on his food.

She nodded, filling his plate up with, macaroni, mashed potatoes, and a dinner roll. When she got to the vegetables, she stopped mid scoop. "You want vegetables, Duke?"

"No."

"Yeah, he does." Nas and I answered at the same time.

"I don't like those." Duke looked to Noelle.

"Okay, we'll since you had fruit you should get pass on veggies today."

Nas chuckled.

"Is that alright, Mommy?" Noelle asked for my consent, still holding the spoon.

I cut my eyes at Duke. He usually didn't get a say in whether or not he had to eat vegetables. But it seemed like around Nas, and now with Noelle, I was outnumbered. If I made him eat the veggies I would look like the bad guy.

"Just this once, Bean," I stressed, giving him a look.

"Bean?" Noelle asked, placing his plate in front of him.

Nas picked up the plate in front of me. "That's what a said, Ma. She trippin'."

She chuckled. "It's cute. Is it a nickname only for you?"

by *Nique Luarks*

A lump formed in my throat. "Uh, actually, it's the nickname my mom gave me growing up. So, I kind of just passed it down." I could feel Nas' eyes on me.

"That's sweet." Noelle beamed. "Does, she still calls you that?"

My chest tightened. "She passed away when I was three months pregnant with Duke." I stared at my son. "But she did up until she died." My eyes found Noelle's sympathetic ones.

"I'm sorry about your loss, Jaime," she empathized. "How did she pass?"

"Ma…" Nas shook his head at her. "Baby, what do you want to eat?" he asked me.

"No, it's fine." I offered a weak smile. I was sure he'd never asked me because he didn't know how. Behind all that hardness, I could see the soft spot he had for me in his eyes. "My dad's best friend murdered her in an argument."

Noelle sighed sadly. "That's really sad, Jaime. You know if you ever need somebody to talk to, you can get my number from Nasir." She picked up the plate in front of her. "I lost my mother when I was fifteen."

"Oh wow, Noelle—"

"Oh, I've dealt with it for a long time, honey." She started piling some kind of pasta onto her plate the same time Nas began filling my mine with macaroni.

"I know how hard that can be."

She nodded. "I think the only death I've taken harder than hers was my son's. His name was Nahmir."

"Ma…" Nas sat my plate down. "Chill, yo. What you on?" The hurt he was trying to hide was evident in his tone.

"Nas—"

"I ain't come over here for all that," he snapped.

Noelle looked at him sadly. "I'm sorry." Quickly wiping the corner of her eye, she placed her smile back on Duke. "So, Duke, you like cake?" She stood up.

"Yeah!" Duke was hyped.

"You like ice cream?" Noelle placed her hands on her hips.

"Strawberry." He pushed his plate away.

"Okay, one piece of cake and strawberry ice cream coming right up, for Nana Noelle's new favorite person." She left the room.

"My bad about Moms. She's nosy as hell." Nas looked over at me with a dispirited look on his handsome face.

Rubbing the side of his face, I leaned in and kissed him gently on the lips. "Did I tell you how fine you are today?"

The corners of his mouth lifted just a little. But for me that was enough. Kissing him again, I pulled back when I felt someone enter the dining room from behind me.

"Where's Mama?" Nikki, Nas' older sister asked, taking a seat in the chair next to Duke.

"In the kitchen." Nas ran his hand down his face and sighed. My baby was thinking hard.

I rubbed his back.

"So what happened last night?" She looked me up and down quickly and then looked back to Nas.

"A bunch of bullshit."

"So, you cool with Ava getting hit over the head with a bottle?" She was speaking like the one who'd knocked Ava's ass over the head wasn't sitting at the table with her.

"Nikki—"

"Okay, Duke..." Noelle returned. "With sprinkles on top, especially for you." She sat the bowl down in front of him.

"What ya'll in here talking about? Jaime, you already met Nikki?" Noelle nodded her head towards her daughter, who looked more like her sister.

169

"We were just getting acquainted." I mustered up a fake smile to give to Nikki out of respect for Nas and his mother.

"I've seen her around." Nikki started loading her plate with food.

"Jaime, Nikki and I go have brunch and do some shopping in the city every Sunday. You should come this week."

"Ma, I thought that was a mother-daughter thing." Nikki stared at her mother like she'd stabbed her in the back.

"Jaime is family, so she's invited." Noelle gave her a stern *don't-fuck-with-me* look.

"Whatever." She started eating.

Noelle nodded her head. "Duke, how's the cake?" She began to finish making her plate.

"It's good." He smacked loudly.

"Nana Noelle can burn, can't she?" she asked, smiling as if he knew what she meant.

"Yep." He nodded.

"You're going to have to come out here more often." She looked to me. "You must be special. Nas never comes to see me anymore."

I stared at the side of Nas' face. "Why not?"

"Because he's a man and they make everything harder than it needs to be." She called him out, taking a hefty bite of greens.

I'd noticed he'd been real quiet since his brother had been mentioned. The sad look on his face didn't go unnoticed as he stared intensely at the table. If we were alone, I would've sat on his lap and kissed him all over. I wasn't used to him wearing his emotions on his face. Nasir was hurting just like everybody else.

"We'll try to get him up here once a week." I grabbed my baby's hand and caressed it softly.

Chapter Fourteen

I found my way again

Ryan

Drying my hair off with a towel, I bent down to look under the bathroom sink for the hairdryer. When I found it, I plugged it up and tossed the towel into the guest bedroom I'd borrowed from Kenya. For the most part, my six-month stay in Kansas City had flown by. It was nice to go somewhere and not know anybody. In New York the family had shit on lock. The guys were like hood royalty and shit.

I won't lie, though. Even though it was peaceful here, I couldn't make it permanent. It was a nice way to jump start a new me, but Missouri wasn't it. Moving out west didn't seem like a bad idea either. It was clear across the country, but I could make do. I'd even thought about going up north.

Turning the volume up on the red Beats pill on the sink, I sang along with Jhene Aiko. Combing through my hair, I contemplated on getting a weave. The ringing of the doorbell pulled me away from the mirror and out of the bathroom.

Humming, I sauntered down the stairs to unlock and open the door. Assuming it was Ms. Lenora, a smiled graced my face. However, it dropped when I came face to face with Silas.

He licked his lips.

A cold gust of wind stiffened my nipples in my white shirt. Crossing my arms, I regretted not putting a bra on. "What?"

"Long time no speak." He smirked.

"I know right?" I'd hadn't spoken one word to him since Quan's sudden pop up. I'd see him going to and from Lenora's but that was about it. Thanksgiving had come and gone. Christmas and New Years had too. It was the second week of January so he was the last person I had expected to see.

"Can I come in?"

I looked behind me. "Yeah, I got a minute. I was kind of in the middle of something." I opened the door wider for him.

"You ain't fuckin' wit' the kid?" He chuckled.

I frowned.

"You take off running every time you see me. What? You avoiding me?" This was the first time I'd really gotten a look at him without his hat on. Silas was too damn fine. Waiting on my answer, he tilted his head to the side.

"What you expect? For me to be chasing you down just because we fucked?" I wasn't built like most women. Sex didn't have to be tied to feelings and emotions. Even though I'd only been with Quan, I could separate the two. Plus Ava had set a good example.

"Shit, I mean at least acknowledge a nigga."

"Is that why you came over here?" I ran my hands through my damp hair.

"Damn, it's like that?" He shook his head. "Naw, Moms wanted me to tell you she was leaving for the weekend."

"I knew that." This particular weekend was all Ms. Lenora had been talking about since the beginning of the year. She and her sister were going to California for a week. They went every year around the same time and this year they were staying at a resort.

"Well, she's gone and she wanted me to give you this." He handed me a single key. "She needs somebody to feed the fish in her room."

I took the key from him. "And why can't you do it? You over there enough."

He smiled. "What's your beef wit' me? You been trippin' since I met you."

"I have low tolerance for men."

Silas laughed. "Just feed the fish, a'ight?" He shook his head walking back towards the door.

Trekking behind him, I rolled my eyes. "I'll think about it."

Opening the door he faced me. "It's something different about you."

"What?" I looked up at him confused.

"Your energy is different."

This time it was my turn to laugh. "My energy? What? You read cards for a living?"

He chuckled. "Nah, man. You got a lil' glow to you. That's all I'm saying."

"Yeah, okay." I held the door as he stepped on the porch.

"Stay up, Ry." He headed towards his Audi. Once he pulled off, I shut the door and locked it.

Jhene Aiko could still be heard playing as I climbed the stairs. Back in the bathroom I stared at my reflection, looking for the glow Silas claimed I had. Turning on the hairdryer, I examined my features. I bobbed my head slowly to the beat, taking a sip of the red wine I'd had waiting for me.

COVERED IN YOUR LOVE 2
by *Nique Luarks*

I had my own personal little concert going when my phone fucked up my whole vibe. Putting my glass down, I picked up my iPhone. Seeing it was Blaze, I grinned.

"B, what's good, Mama?"

"Shit, you tell me?" Quan's deep voice seeped through the speaker.

"Really?" I couldn't believe Blaze would do me like that.

"So, you not gon' unblock me, Ry?"

"Unblock you for what? I don't fuck with you like that?" I combed through my hair.

"Why not? I thought we were family." The amusement in his scruffy baritone didn't go unnoticed.

"Speaking of family…" I smirked.

"Here you go."

"Don't you have one to attend to? Why are you calling me? There's a reason I blocked your number." I sat the comb down and the wineglass took its place in my hand.

"I am attending to my family. What you think this is smart ass?"

"You being annoying," I shot back.

"And that would make you what? Irritating?" He chuckled.

"If I'm so irritating then why are you calling me?"

"I told you why. I ain't heard from you in a minute and I wanted to make sure you were straight."

"You couldn't have just asked Blaze?" That would've been better than a phone call. I rolled my eyes.

"I wanted to hear it from you."

"Whatever. Tell Blaze I thought we were better than that." It wasn't like her to out me. She was usually team Ryan.

"She don't know I got her phone. Kai Money snatched it up for me."

"This is borderline stalking."

"Only for you."

"Ugh, are you flirting with me?" I grinned, taking a sip from the glass.

"How am I doin'?"

"Quit while you're ahead." I snickered, putting the glass down to plug up the flat irons.

He chuckled. "Fuck you, punk."

I laughed.

"I miss you." His voice softened.

My mood shifted almost immediately. Leaning against the threshold, I stared absentmindedly at the floor. After we'd had sex in the Phantom, he reluctantly had the driver drop me back off at my hotel. We were both smart enough to know sex couldn't clean up the mess he had made. We hadn't spoken since.

"You ain't gotta say it back." He broke the silence. "Long as you know I do. And I know you miss me too. But I fucked up, so now I gotta live with whatever happens next."

My stomach churned.

"Look, Blaze found out about her phone." He chuckled. "Kenya's ole snitching ass."

"Hey, Ry!"I heard Kenya in the background.

"You here her?" Quan asked.

"Hey, Ken!" I cheesed. After the incident at the club, we'd all been thick as thieves. Well, everybody except for Ava. She wasn't talking to anyone. Not even Blaze.

"Girl, I Facetimed you. Quan got you on speaker." She gave the head's up.

"I'ma let ya'll have it," he announced. "Ryan!"

"Yeah?"

"I love you."

The line went quiet. Resting my head against the threshold, I sighed.

"Ry, girl, I Facetimed you because I wanted your opinion on something," Kenya started as I began parting my hair.

"I was at school. What's up?"

"Girl, so tell me why I done gained another three pounds. If Cole got me pregnant again I'ma whoop his ass," she fussed.

Staring at my reflection, I smiled. Suddenly, I saw the glow Silas was talking about. I was genuinely happy with myself. I'd come a long way from long days and sleepless nights. I was putting me first and it felt good. The shit felt great.

Quan

Four days later…

"Are you serious?!" Brianna screamed.

"Dead ass." I kicked my feet up on the end table and started scrolling through my messages. "And quit yellin',crazy-ass broad." I glanced up at her.

"How can you say that to me?" Her bottom lip trembled.

"Because I want a fuckin' DNA test, Brianna. I been and told you that. Ain't shit changed but the season." Logging onto Draya's Facebook, I went to Ryan's page.

"So, why go to all my doctor's appointments if you think there's a chance she might not be yours?"

"Because if she is mine, and I wasn't there, it'll fuck with me." I saw Ry had uploaded a recent picture. Clicking on it, I licked my lips.

Damn.

"What are you looking at?" Brianna tried to snatch my phone out of my hand. "What bitch got you cheesing?"

I brought my foot down and leaned forward. "Brianna, I choke slam bitches. Quit trying me, yo." Sitting my phone face up on the table, I stood up.

COVERED IN YOUR LOVE 2
by *Nique Luarks*

She cowered as I towered over her frame. "Quan, why..." She choked up. "Why do you treat me so bad?" She started crying.

Yo...

Sitting back down on the couch, I placed my head in my hands. Brianna's ass was too emotional. And it wasn't because of the pregnancy either. She'd always been an emotional fuckin' wreck. Picking my phone back up, I studied Ryan's picture. The caption read *Bundle Withdrawals.*

I chuckled at her goofy ass. It was no secret Ry loved those long-ass weaves. That's why I was so surprised to see her rockin' her real hair. Not caring that I was using Draya's account, I commented under the photo.

Draya GetToIt : I like your hair short.

"DaQuan, what can I do?" Brianna was still crying and whining.

"Give me a DNA test when the baby is born."

Ry commented back under her picture.

Ryan Mariah : Thank you girl. You know me though.

"I'm telling you it's your baby."

"Brianna, get out of my face." I turned the TV on.

by *Nique Luarks*

Draya GetToIt: I like your long hair too. Especially when I'm pulling that shit.

Ryan Mariah: ...Quan.

I laughed at the eye rolling emoji she used.

Draya GetToIt: just checkin' in wit you.

Ryan Mariah: Bye loser.

"When did you get a Facebook? Why didn't you add me?" Brianna sat down next to me.

Draya GetToIt: That mouth gon get you in trouble. Keep on Ry.

Ryan Mariah: I don't miss.

I smiled, shaking my head at her tough ass.

"You got me so fucked up." Brianna hopped up and stormed out of the room.

Draya GetToIt: You a driver Ry, you ain't no shooter.

Ryan Mariah: how did that arm heal? Can you bend it all the way yet?

I laughed, thinking back to my last trip to Dallas. Ry's ass shot me in the arm close range. Then her crazy ass turned the gun on Nas for trying to cover for me. The minute she saw I was bleeding out, her ass panicked, though. The make-up sex after that was wild as fuck.

Draya GetToIt: Aight scrub. You got it. I shoulda pressed charges

She sent back the rat and laughing emoji.

Logging out of Draya's Facebook, I tossed my phone on the couch next to me. Flipping through the channels, I heard Brianna slamming shit in the kitchen. Turning the TV up, I continued to surf channels until I stopped on CNN. That short conversation with Ry was enough to get me through a couple days. Content, I relaxed against the throw pillows and closed my eyes.

Chapter Fifteen

Family first…

Nas

"Where's Ava?" Kai asked, coming in with Blaze on his heels.

"Hey, Nas." She smiled.

"Sup, sis?" Leaning back in my seat, I looked to Kai Money. "She ain't here yet."

Blaze had somehow talked Kai into playing mediator with Ava and me. He didn't give a fuck either way as long business was still handled. Blaze wasn't having it, though, because apparently, Ava had distanced herself from everybody. Running my hands down my face, I sat up. I had better shit to do. Duke and I needed shape ups.

Blaze took her phone out of her purse. "Let me call her." As soon as those words left her mouth, Ava came strolling in with shades on her face. At first, I thought it was because she had a black eye or something. Then I remembered how extra Ava was. She was bougie as fuck. That was her style, though.

Removing her coat, she took a seat at the table. "Can we make this quick? I got shit to do." She took her sunglasses off.

"Ava, really?" Blaze grimaced. "Why are you acting like that?"

"Blaze, don't act dumb because—"

"Watch it—" Kai cut her off.

"Ya'll let that bitch sneak me." Her eyes landed on me. "I thought it was family first."

"Ain't nobody let that girl sneak you, yo." I had loosened my grip on Jaime thinking I had the situation under control. I didn't think she was so strong and quick. By the time I was able to grab her, Ava had already hit the floor.

"So, why did ya'll have Dom take me home? Why didn't you make sure I was straight?" Ava looked directly at Blaze.

"If you would've answered your phone you would've known we got into a fight." Blaze explained. "You know I would never leave you hanging."

"This is some sappy-ass shit." I sighed, irritated. Females do too much.

Kai chuckled and I knew it was because the only reason he was sitting through this was to appease his wife.

"So, you're going to keep fuckin' with her?" Ava glared at me.

"Yeah." I stared back at her. "What the fuck do it have to do wit' you?" She didn't act like this when Blaze and Kenya came around. Shit, she was cordial as fuck with Tami *and* Myeisha. Whatever issue she had with Jaime was personal.

"You acting like you love the girl or something." She sat up straight in her seat.

"And if I do?"

"How!?" She damn near jumped out of her seat. "You haven't known her that long."

"Man…" I drawled, waving her off.

"You didn't even run her by me." She looked hurt for real.

Resting my elbows on the table, I shook my head. "Yo, Ava, you acting like we fuckin' or somethin'."

"I was about to ask." Kai looked amused.

"Man, nah." Ava was like a for real little sister. We had that one close encounter, but I stopped that shit. She was more of a sister to me than Nikki was. She'd hustled on the block right along with me and Quan. Not even no drunk shit could make me accidentally take it there with Ava.

"Ugh, hell no." Her face contorted into a disgusted look. "I just thought we were better than that."

"Quit acting like a brat, man." I now knew what the issue was. Ava was used to being my favorite girl. Spoiled ass.

She gave me a evil look. "You could've at least let me sit down and meet her. Like at lunch or something. You don't even care I might not like her." She pouted.

"Oh Lord." Blaze sighed. "Really Ava?"

Kai pushed away from the table. "Blaze meet me in my office." Standing up, he left the room.

Blaze stood up. "Answer the phone when I call you, crazy." She shook her head, picking up her purse. "And what you mean you *might* not like her. She clocked your ass over the head with a bottle." Blaze giggled, making her exit.

Ava snickered. "Fuck you, bitch." She sat on the table. "And you…" She pointed at me with one of her long-ass nails and rolled her neck. "Don't act brand new."

"I didn't know I needed an okay from you, Ava." Standing up, I threw a balled-up piece of paper at her. I waited as she put her coat and sunglasses back on.

"Well, now you know. Now, call Jaime and tell her we're going to happy hour." She led the way out of the room.

"Nah."

"Why? I promise I'ma be good."

"I know how you are with that fuckin' taser." I would hate to have to beat Ava's ass behind Jaime.

"Here." She unzipped her purse and went inside it. "Take it." She handed me her taser.

Taking it from her, I pressed the button on the elevator. "You gon' do a bid one day, yo."

"So, are you going to call her?"

"I might." We stepped on the elevator.

"So, you're really diggin' her, huh?" She hit the button for the ground floor.

"Yeah, I fucks wit' her."

"Why *her*? I've seen you go through a bunch of bitches. You don't even like chicks with kids." She tittered.

"She different."

"Wow." She faced forward.

"Wow, what?" The doors opened.

Ava stepped out first. "You care about something other than the streets and money."

"Is that a bad thing?"

"No. I'm just all alone now." She sighed. Ava was a softer version of me, so I knew exactly what she meant. Ava was tough as shit and didn't let nobody in her personal space.

"Man, cut that shit out." We walked through the corridor.

"Whatever." She switched next to me. "Just tell that hoe to be ready in the next hour and a half. I got shit to do."

"If I do this and you start trippin', you gon' have to leave New York, Ava." She was family so I wouldn't kill her, but I'd beat the fuck out of her.

"Boy, you ain't running me away from nowhere." She waved me off. "Open the door," she ordered as we came up on the double glass doors.

Pushing the door open, I let it go as soon as my right foot hit the pavement.

"Ouch!" Ava yelped, pushing through the door. "You could've broken my nose or chipped my damn tooth!" She held her face.

"Good." I swaggered to my whip.

"Asshole. Tell Jaime she got one hour." She made her way to her grey 2017 BMW.

Jaime

"Say what?!" I looked at Nasir like he had two heads.

"Ava wanna link with you." He took a hot chip out the bag Duke was holding.

"Why? So I can knock her ass out again?" I picked up one of Duke's toys.

"Nah, she ain't on that type of time."

"Are you coming?" I handed Duke the toy. "Take this to your room please."

"I'm chillin'." He leaned back coolly next to Nas.

"What did yo mama say, lil' nigga?" Nas looked down at him.

Duke sighed loudly. "Ya'll always tell me to do stuff," he pouted, scooting off the sofa.

We watched him stump out of the living room.

"That lil' nigga bad." Nas stood up. "We bout to be out, though."

Nas took Duke to the barbershop every Wednesday with him. I took that time to face a blunt, get some school work done, and clean up after Duke and Nas. It was guaranteed alone time and I was grateful for it.

"Okay."

"So, you going, right?" he pressed, hovering over me.

"I don't want to."

"Not even for me?" He picked me up.

Wrapping my legs around his waist and my arms around his neck, I gazed into his eyes. When he planted a wet kiss on my lips, I slid my tongue in his mouth, and he palmed my ass.

by *Nique Luarks*

Sucking on his bottom lip, I started grinding slowly against him. He pulled away smiling.

"Yo lil' freaky ass." Shaking his head, he put me down. "Go holler at my sis, a'ight?"

"If I go, I'm not staying long." I gave in.

"Bet. Duke!" He went and stood at the bottom of the stairs. Opening the hallway closet, I removed Duke's coat. "Where is she trying to meet at?"

"Knowing Ava, somewhere where happy hour is live and drinks are strong as fuck."

Duke came running down the stairs talking on the phone.

"What your moms say about running on the stairs, dude?" Nas rubbed the top of the Duke's head.

"Dad, I talk to you later. Bye." He started to hang up. "Okay." Walking over to me, he handed me his phone.

"What?"

"He wanna talk to you."

Taking the phone from him, I put it to my ear. Before I could utter a word, Nas snatched it out of my hand. Pressing end, he handed Duke his phone back. Shaking my head, I helped Duke into his coat and put his skully on. Reaching back into the closet, I took out my parka and closed the door.

"What was all that for?" I slipped my arms through the jacket.

"What he need to talk to you about?" He opened the door for us. Grabbing my purse, I followed Duke outside. Once Nas shut the door, I locked it and we started down the stairs.

"Probably wanted to talk about Duke's birthday." I shrugged, hitting the unlock button on my key fob. Stopping at Nas'

charger, I opened the door for Duke. "His birthday is in two
weeks."

"You wasn't gon' tell me?" Pulling me close, he wrapped his
arms around me.

"You would've found out eventually."

"When? At the birthday party?" He kissed my forehead. "Go get
in the car. I'm bout to have Ava call you now."

He stood on the sidewalk and waited for me to get in. Once I
had my jeep running, I got an incoming call.

"Hello?"

"Jaime, this is Ava. Can you meet me at Bar 54?"

Pulling my seatbelt across my body, I pulled away from the
curb. "Yeah, I'm on my way now." Nas honked twice as I
passed his car.

***

I swear if Ava starts some shit, I will gladly finish it.
Stepping into the restaurant, it didn't take me long to find her
sitting at the bar. She was looking down at her phone so she
didn't see me approach her.

"What's up?" I placed my purse in the seat between us and sat
down.

"Sup?" She waved the bartender down. "Let me get two double
tequila sunrises."

"Coming right up."

"I didn't think you were going to come." She sat her phone

down.

"I wasn't at first. I'm only doing this for Nas."

She looked me up and down. "Well, that's one thing we have in common. At least we're off to a good start."

" A better start would've been you apologizing." I frowned. Ava was way too pretty to have an attitude like the one she had.

"Girl, I'm not apologizing to you. Bitch, did you forget you almost gave me brain damage with a fuckin' Cîroc bottle." She side eyed me.

"Then why did you ask me to come here, Ava?"

The bartender slid our drinks in front of us.

"Thanks."

"This better be strong too." Ava took a long sip.

"Ava, don't start no shit today." He shook his head at her before walking to the other end of the bar.

"You hang out here often?" I sipped slowly.

"Three times a week."

"Mmmm."

"So, back to what I was saying. I feel like we're even so we ain't gotta do all that sentimental shit." She took her gum out of her mouth and placed it on the rim of her glass.

"You threw a bottle at me." *Was this girl serious?*

"You had too much mouth." She shrugged. "Plus I was drunk as fuck. And you could've given me a concussion." She paused to take another sip.

"I should've." I drank from my glass.

"You know how fuckin' thick a Cîroc bottle is? I wanted to beat your ass all week." She continued sipping.

"So, this is you?" I was starting to see Ava had no filter. I don't know why I was surprised, though. The company she kept was rough. I hadn't known Nas and his boys that long, but I knew gansters and drug dealers when I saw them.

She laughed. "Love me or leave me." Shrugging, she stared at me. "You cute, though. I guess Nas did okay."

"*Okay*?" I chuckled. Getting comfortable, I took a long sip out from my straw.

"I mean, I wouldn't allow my brothers to be with nothing but the best."

"You give them a hard time like you do me?"

"Nope." She exaggerated the *p*. "I'm close to them all, but Nas is like my twin. Kai went to prison, Quan had Ry, and I just met Cole for the first time three years ago."

"So, you haven't known Blaze and Kenya long?"

She finished off her drink. "Nah. But that's family. Plus, since Blaze been around, she keeps the peace. Like that's her role or something. Kai is the big boss and she's boss lady. Kenya is the fun one. She keeps everybody laughing."

She waved the bartender back over.

"And Ryan is with Quan?" I downed the rest of my drink.

"Not no more," she pouted. "Gerald, let me get two more and two shots of tequila. Don't forget my lime either."

He only shook his head at her before making her request.

"I don't drink like that." I was only a social drinker and more of a smoker. It was five in the evening. Way too early for me to be getting drunk. I had a three-year-old that couldn't be left alone for more than two minutes.

"Don't be acting like that." She grinned as Gerald put our shots on the counter. "But back to what I was saying." She turned sideways in her chair to face me. "Ryan is the muscle. She will beat a bitch, choke a bitch, stab a bitch, shoot a bitch, drown a bitch, and run a bitch over," she explained, counting playfully with her fingers.

I laughed before sipping from the new glass Gerald had put in front of me.

Ava giggled. "I'm serious, yo." She took a long sip from her straw. "She had to fight a lot growing up because of her looks." She shrugged, still sipping.

"And what role do *you* play in the clique?" I grabbed for my tequila shot and lime.

Ava picked hers up as well. "I'm the wanderer." After taking her shot, she bit down on her lime.

I did the same with mine. "That's interesting." I sat my shot glass down.

"How so?" She started drinking from her glass.

"That must mean you change your mind a lot." I shrugged, stating the obvious.

"I do." She sighed. "But I always come back to what I know to be solid."

"Which is the family?"

"Yeah. Kai saw I was heading down the wrong path after I graduated high school." She paused to take a drink. "He made me get a business degree. Some stupid shit about him wanting to instill some stability into my life." Shrugging, she finished off the rest of her drink. "Whatever the fuck that means."

"So, you handle all business ventures."

She nodded. "Their business and mine."

"What kind of business do you own?" I sipped.

"Two tattoo parlors." Her face lit up. "They're my babies."

"That's what's up." I smiled. "I'ma have to come and get some ink."

"Where you tatted?"

"My back. I got a memorial for my mom."

"Why your back? Nobody can see it." She put her gum back in her mouth.

"Because she always had my back." I finished off my drink. "Even when I didn't know she was looking out." My mama was hard topic for me to touch on, and now was definitely not the time to be confiding in Ava. She hated me.

"That's dope." She nodded, giving me her stamp of approval. "I wish I was bold enough to get tatted."

I bucked my eyes. "What? You don't have any?" How could she own a tattoo shop but not have one? Wasn't that like a rule? If you worked at a tattoo parlor you were expected to look the part.

"Not one. That's not my thing. Don't get me wrong. They're sexy, but I don't want them." She rubbed her hand across her arm.

"That's different."

She shrugged. "Anywho, thanks for coming out. I missed my family. Cutting them off because I was mad at you backfired on my dumb ass." She snickered, reaching for her jacket.

"Thank you for giving me a fair chance." I chuckled.

"You must've knocked some sense into my ass." She giggled, going into her purse. Placing a few bills onto the counter, she put her purse strap on her shoulder. "Next time drinks are on you."

I smiled.

"Just pop some gum in your mouth." She spoke over her shoulder, walking towards the exit. "That way, they'll never know you're not sober."

I laughed, putting my parka on. Being a psychology major made me read between the lines of what people said. Sitting here with Ava made me realize her issue wasn't with me. It was with the changes she was going through. It wasn't just her, Ry, and the boys anymore. She now had to share them all.

Grabbing my bag, I left out of the restaurant. Ava wasn't that bad of a person once you actually got to know her. She was just a free spirit who lived in the moment. The effects of the liquor were starting to wear down as I started my jeep. I was in the mood for one thing and one thing only: Nas' sex.

Scrolling to his name in my contacts, I pulled up our messages.

Me: What are you doing?

Starting the car, I put my seatbelt on.

Nasir: Chillin wit my folks. What's up?

Me: I miss you.

Backing out of the parking space, I started my journey home.

Nasir: I miss you too baby

Coming to a stop at a red light, I smiled so hard I'm surprised my cheeks didn't get stuck.

Me: Come show me how much.

I took off again. I wanted Nas in the worst way. The way he handled by body was Grammy-award worthy. The liquor only intensified my need for his touch. I was feigning for just a simple kiss.

Nasir: I'm on my way.

Chapter Sixteen

If you never learn, you'll never know a good thing...

Ryan

I entered the house with two hands full of groceries. Closing the door with my foot, I stumbled to the kitchen and let the bags slip from my fingers. Rubbing my sore hands, I stepped around the bags and went to the sink to wash my hands. After drying them off, I went for my ringing phone. Seeing it was a Facetime from Blaze, I answered.

"What's up, chick?" I removed my joint from my purse.

"My Ry..."

My attention snapped back to my phone. Pressing end with a frown on my face, I lit my blunt. I didn't want to have to block Blaze, but she was a bit too loose with her phone. Neither she nor Kai believed in passwords so Kai had easy access to it. Him taking her phone and passing it off to Quan was pissing me off.

After taking a toke of the weed, I started putting the groceries away. Halfway through my blunt, I was high and had cut the Bluetooth speaker in the kitchen on. Vibing to the music, I sang along with my girl, Yuna. Putting the blunt out, I went in my purse for a piece of gum. Finishing up the on the groceries, I went for my phone when a text alert went off.

Blaze: check the mail My Ry

Staring at the text from Quan, I frowned. Sitting my phone down, I went to the front door where the mail drop was. Bending over I picked the mail up and rummaged through the mail. It was all pretty much junk mail. However, a red envelope caught my eye. The sender read *DaQuan Harris.*

Tearing it open, I removed a paper that was folded over twice. Quan's handwriting sat neatly on the page.

"*My Ry,*

I'm writing this letter since this is the only way I can reach you without going through other muthafuckas. It's cool, though. This shit brings me back to when I went to prison for two years and you held me down. Your letters were the only thing getting me through that shit. Your visits too. The whole time I thought about what I would do if you ever left me.

Now here I am without you. And you know what ya boy did? I cried like a baby. You not wanting shit to do with me is breaking my heart, man cause I know it's my fault. You ain't ever did nothing but love me and be my rider.

Anyway, I'ma write you until you take me off the block list. I'ma call you too. Kai Money be coming through."

I chuckled.

"I love you Ryan, and I ain't gon' stop. I don't want you to stop loving me either."

I sighed and folded the paper back up. Heading back into the kitchen with the envelope still in hand, I went straight for my blunt. Why did he always have to complicate shit? Of course, I would always love him and of course, I knew the feeling was mutual. Nothing in this world could change that.

Relighting my blunt, I turned my music on and busied myself with finding something to cook for dinner. Seeing Blaze's number cross my screen again, I stopped what I was doing. Already knowing who it was, I answered with an attitude.

"What, DaQuan?"

"It's Blaze this time." She giggled on the other end. "I'ma fight Mehkai."

Ashing the blunt, I put it out. "Tell your husband to mind his own business and stay out of mine."

"Will do. Quan said you hung up on him."

"I did. I don't know why he won't just leave me alone." The whole point of me blocking him was for him not to be able to reach out to me.

"Because even though he screwed up, he loves and misses you." Mother Hen started, making me snicker. Blaze was the most positive person I'd ever met. Looking at her from the outside, you wouldn't think she would knock a bitch out or that she was married to a ruthless nigga like Kai Money. Blaze was the very definition of *don't judge a book by its cover*.

"Too bad for him. He could've kept his bullshit-ass letter, though." Taking the grapes out of the refrigerator, I went to the sink to wash them off.

"He sent you a letter?" I could hear the smile in her voice.

"Girl, yeah. Ava probably wrote it," I joked. I knew Quan wrote it because I recognized his handwriting, but Ava was known for doing their dirty work when it came to women.

She giggled. "I'm about to call her ass on three way and ask."

I chuckled, hopping up on the sink. "A'ight, I'm about to call Kenya." Dialing Kenya up, I waited for her to answer before I merged her in.

"Ry, what's going on?"

"Hey, Ken," Blaze spoke first.

"What's up, bitch?" Ava's loud ass blasted through the speaker.

"The whole gang is here. What happened?" Kenya asked.

"Right? Which one of them niggas cheated?" Ava sniggled.

We all laughed.

Tossing a plump, green grape into my mouth, I chewed slowly. "Quan sent me a letter."

"What it say? The baby ain't his?"

"No, Ava. I'm pretty sure the baby is his."

"How do you know for a fact?"

"Kenya, why would he claim a baby if he wasn't sure it was his?" Blaze chimed in, answering for me.

"Exactly." I agreed one hundred percent with Blaze.

"Girl, its two sides to every story, so shut up." Ava smacked her lips. "Ryan needs to quit acting like Brianna ain't no jump off."

"I never said she wasn't. But I won't act like he wasn't fuckin' with her heavy. Buying her shit and spending nights with her." I chomped down on another grape. I knew Quan like the back of my hand. If he was claiming a baby, there was over a ninety percent chance he was the daddy.

COVERED IN YOUR LOVE 2
by *Nique Luarks*

"So, let me ask you this, Ry," Blazed cut in. "If Quan didn't have a baby on the way, would you consider taking him back?"

"Yep," Ava chirped.

"Excuse you, Ava." I chuckled. "I'm pretty sure that question was intended for *me*." Clearing my throat, I shrugged. "If I'ma be real wit' ya'll, I really don't know. A part of me feels like I've taught him a lesson, the other part—the biggest part—is saying he won't ever change."

We all sat silent after that. As women, love was always harder on us than on men. They could do a million and one things to hurt us and expect forgiveness before the day was done. They took advantage of our kindness and used our love for them as our weakness. I was tired of being a pushover.

"Just come back home, Ry." Ava broke the silence. "Even if you don't take Quan's ugly ass back, come home. Ain't shit for you in Missouri. Wait...unless you still smashin' Sy."

"Biiiiitch, you still fuckin' ole boy," Kenya's nosy ass asked.

"No, I'm—"

"I knew it!" Ava cut me off.

"Ava, you don't know shit." I swung my legs, shaking my head at her. "I'm not smashin' him. That was a one-and-done situation."

205

"I agree with Ava, Ry." The calmness in Blaze's voice stopped our bickering. "Your family is here. You can come work at the center part-time and show some of the girls how to make themselves up. I'll even see if I can request you only for all my shoots."

Blaze owned a non-profit youth center where urban kids came to learn how to read, write, and draw. When she wasn't at a photo shoot or being a mommy and a wife, she was there. She'd just opened it at the beginning of the year, but in our recent conversations, she'd told me the kids loved it. But hearing she could get me in the door to the big league's piqued my interest. New York was known for fashion, and where there was fashion, there was makeup.

"That's dope, Blaze," Ava piped in.

I nodded in agreement because it was. For Blaze to consider me being her makeup artist when she could do makeup was all love.

"Just think about it," Blaze pressed.

"I will," I promised.

"Soooo…" Ava started. "While I got the whole gang here, I might as well tell y'all I went and had drinks with Jaime."

"What?" Kenya drawled. "Ya'll didn't fight did ya'll?"

"Nah, she was actually cool. I can see why Nas fucks with her."

"I still can't believe she knocked your ass out." I laughed, putting the grapes back in the fridge.

"Ava shouldn't have thrown that bottle at her."

"Oh, chill, Mother Hen." Ava sucked her teeth. "We good now. Ya'll, I think Nas is really in love. What kind of voodoo did you hoes put on my brothers?"

"I don't know about voodoo." Kenya cleared her throat. "But I'm about to go put this pussy on Cole, so I'll talk to ya'll later."

"That's why you probably pregnant now." Ava chortled.

"Whatever, bye."

"Blaze, you cook?" Ava asked. "I'm on my way over."

"Kai hasn't eaten yet."

"And?"

"And I need to make sure my husband eats first."

I snickered.

"Well, I'm on my way anyway. I need to tell Kai something."

"Okay. Ry, I'll talk to you later. Think about what I said."

"Blaze, wait," Ava said hurriedly before she could hang up. "What kind of tequila ya'll got over there? Do I need to stop at the store?"

Blaze smacked her lips. "I'll see you in a minute, Ava. Later Ry."

"Bye, Keyshia." Ava laughed.

"One." I shook my head, exiting the kitchen. I cut the lights off on the way out.

I was halfway up the stairs when I stopped in my tracks. Backtracking, I ended up back in the kitchen. Moving through the dark until I reached the island, I picked up the red envelope. Making my way back upstairs, I opened the letter back up to read it again.

Jaime

"Happy birthday to yoooouu!...." Everyone surrounding Duke sang in unison as he wrapped his arms around Nas' neck as he held him.

"Make a wish, Bean!" I beamed, rubbing his back.

"I don't want to," he pouted, laying his face on Nas' chest.

"Don't be acting like that, Duke!" Jaylen was holding her phone to take a picture. "Say cheese."

"He don't feel good." Nas looked down at me. "He's running a fever and shit."

"You sick, Duke?" Shane sat down in the chair that Duke was supposed to be standing on.

"His daddy said he got a fever." Maxx wrapped her arms around my waist.

I blew out Duke's candles for him and everybody clapped as I removed the number four candle and the red, silver, and black ones surrounding it.

"Dang, how many daddies do you have, Duke?" Shane played in Maxx's long hair. "I need me another daddy too." She poked her lips out.

by *Nique Luarks*

"Shut your grown-ass up." Jaylen gave her a stern look. "Matter of fact, all the kids get away from the table while we cut the cake."

All the kids took off running towards the arcade. Jaylen followed behind them.

"I gotta go too?" Tati asked, sitting in Kenya's lap. "I don't even want no cake."

"Go see where your daddy is with your brother." Kenya lifted her off of her lap and she took off.

I'd decided to give Duke a birthday party at Bounce and Play. Nas gave me the money for the food, cake, majority of Duke's gifts and paid for the kids to play unlimited. Troy must've still been mad because he hadn't even called Duke to wish him a happy birthday. Everything was going according to plan and everyone was having a good time. Well, that is everyone except Duke.

When the party first started, my baby laid his head down on the table and cried. At first Nas was hard on him for whining, but after seeing he wasn't feeling good, he'd been babying him. I cut the cake in small squares as Blaze scooped ice cream onto the plates.

"Thank you."

"You're welcome." She smiled. "Duke, okay?"

"Yeah." I moved over so Nas could sit down with him. "You want cake, Bean?"

He shook his head no.

"He got a cold?" Kenya rummaged through the party gift bags of candy taking out all of the Reese's Cups.

"I think so. I'ma give him some medicine when we leave here." Gently rubbing the top of Duke's head, I planted a soft kiss on his forehead. My baby was burning up.

"We bout to ride out in a few." Nas sat his back against the chair. "He needs to lay down."

"Okay." I nodded. "I at least wanna open up the gifts people brought."

"What for? They know what they got him." He frowned. "My lil' nigga don't give a fuck about none of them gifts right now."

"Look at Papa Nas." Ava came out of nowhere holding balloons and a gift bag.

I chuckled. Since we'd hashed out our beef, we'd actually been really cool. It was like a ritual for us to go have drinks every Wednesday. Instead of sitting in the house on that day waiting on Nas and Duke to get back, I now had something to do that I looked forward to. That didn't stop her from bringing up me hitting her with a bottle every chance she got, though.

Sitting the gift bag on the table, she took the vacant seat next to Kenya. "This place smells like germs." She looked around disgusted as kids ran around.

Kenya chuckled. "I can't wait until you have kids."

"I'm too smart for all that."

"What is that supposed to mean?" Blaze stopped scooping.

"Ain't no baby or no nigga locking me down. What I look like?" She looked down at her flawless nails. "Damn, I need a fill."

Blaze only shook her head.

Shane, Tati, and Maxx ran up to the table together.

"Kenya, my daddy said come and change your son." Tati hugged Ava.

"This dude." Kenya pushed her chair away from the table, stood up, and switched away with Tati trailing her.

After passing out cake and ice cream, I sat down next to Nas and a now sleeping Duke. "We should probably get him home. Can you drop us off now?" We had ridden with Nas, and now that I' was thinking about we'd been *staying* with him too since the incident at the club. The only time I'd been home in the past couple weeks was to switch our clothes out.

"Ya'll ain't coming home wit' me?" He rested his arm on the back of the chair behind me.

"We can if you want. I don't want Duke to be a hassle. I know how he gets when he gets sick." I wiped Duke's cheek.

"Hassle?" He frowned. "Yo, Jaime, quit playing wit' me."

"What?" My eyes met his.

"Duke ain't no fuckin' hassle."

"What's wrong wit' Nana Noelle's favorite person?" I smiled at Noelle as she leaned down to plant a kiss on Duke's cheek. She'd gotten here an hour before the party with Nas and me to help set up. I wasn't sure where she'd disappeared to, but she was all smiles now.

"Where the hell you been?" Nas grilled her and I stood up to clear the table.

"I'm not your woman, so I'm not your responsibility." She put her hands on her hip. "Jaime, get your boy."

Blaze giggled.

"I thought you was beefin' wit' yo sister." I looked to Ava who was staring at me.

I shrugged. "We're not talking right now."

"Mama!" Shane jumped up and took off running.

My eyes followed her as she rushed towards Jade and her clique.

No this bitch didn't.

Myeisha was carrying a gift that was wrapped in colorful wrapping paper. Jade stopped to talk to a few of our family members before they headed in our direction. The loud thud on the table made me look back in Ava's direction when she sat her taser down on the table. Blaze turned in her seat so her back wasn't facing them as they approached the table. Jade looked back and forth between Nas and me before she finally spoke.

"I came to wish my nephew a happy birthday. I didn't come to beef." She looked down at Ava's taser.

"Yo, Eisha, why the fuck are you here?" Nas' nostrils flared.

"I was invited." She smirked, sitting the gift on the table. Ava knocked it down.

"Yeah a'ight." Nas stood up. "Sit down and hold Duke." He looked down at me as he passed Duke over.

"Okay, now, hold up," Noelle interfered, stopping Nas. "This is not the time or place for all that ghetto, hood mess. Nasir, this is Duke's day. Don't ruin it."

214

"We weren't staying long anyway." Jade rolled her eyes as Jaylen approached the table with Maxx following her. I assumed Maxx ran to get her because thanks to Jade talking to her and Shane like they were grown, she knew about us fighting in the club.

"Jade, why are you so damn messy?" Jaylen shook her head. They'd settled their differences, but Jaylen still couldn't tolerate her presence for too long.

"Jaylen, go find some fuckin' business." Jade flipped her hair. "Like I said I'm leaving. I know you bitches like to jump. Let's go, ya'll," she addressed her posse. "Oh yeah, Troy said call him," she shot over her shoulder.

What?

Before I could react to her comment, one of the chicks she was with stopped walking and pointed at the table. "Tell Ryan she still gon' have to see me." It was then that I noticed the long mark that started underneath her eye and ended beneath her chin.

Ava jumped up with her taser and moved like lightening, but Nas was quicker than she was and held her back. "Bitch, we don't take threats over here." She struggled to get out of Nas' grasp.

"Ava!" Noelle grabbed her. "These bitches are below you. Now, sit your rowdy ass down." She faced Jade and her crew.

"Thanks for the gifts. You can go now." Turning towards Nas, she pointed her finger in his face. "You, Cole, Kai, and Quan load all this shit up and put it in the car so Duke can go. Did you forget he was sick?"

She snatched her purse up. "I'm getting too old for this shit," Noelle mumbled, making sure she had her keys. "Jaime, call me when Duke gets settled. Are y'all going to Nas' house?" She slipped her leather gloves on.

"Yeah." I looked up at Nas.

"Okay, I'll drop by later on. Call me if you need me before then." Kissing Duke once more on the cheek, she rubbed my arm and made her exit.

As Nas and his boys gathered everything, my thoughts stayed on what Jade had said. What was she doing talking to Troy of all people? Let her tell it, she hated him more than I did. I was sure I was wearing my emotions on my sleeve because Blaze kept asking was I okay. I honestly didn't know how to feel about Jade's comment, but I knew she had me fucked up.

Chapter Seventeen

Love can make you do some crazy things

Ryan

Lying across Lenora's bed, I watched her sort through her wardrobe. It was going on nine, which meant I'd officially been with her all day. After taking her to Costco this morning, we went and got facials. From there, we had lunch and after that, we stopped at the mall for an hour and a half. I was running on E, but somehow, Lenora was charged. I didn't even want to get up and walk across the street.

"You alright?" She tossed a shirt in the donation bin she'd made.

"Yeah, I'm just tired." I yawned, stretching.

"You need to get more sleep, dear."

She was probably right. I used to be able to stay up for twenty-four hours straight and be good. I guess now that I' was getting older, I couldn't hang. The only thing about that was I'd actually been sleeping a lot. It wasn't like I was working a job. My every day activities usually consisted of me going to school and coming home and chilling. I'd go see a movie or go shopping occasionally, but for the most part, I was in the house posted.

"What you think about this one?" She held up a black Gucci sweater. "It's a little tight around my mid-section."

I yawned. "I like that one. Keep it because you can always lose weight."

"You're right." She tossed it with the pile she was keeping.

"Lenora…" I rolled over on my back and looked up at the ceiling.

"Hmmm?"

"How long do you think it's going to take for me to fully get over him?" That was something I would've asked Grammy had she been alive. I needed some kind of reassurance that eventually I would be alright.

"Whenever you're ready to let him go." I felt her sit down on the bed.

"How can I speed up the process?" I sighed, putting my hands behind my head.

Lenora laughed. "Child, please. I wish it was that easy. You know it's okay to forgive, Ry."

I turned my head to look at her.

"Is that what you feel like you want to do?"

"I feel like my love ain't good enough." I shrugged, looking back up at the ceiling. "If I'm not good enough for him, why should he be good enough for me?"

"Do you really believe you aren't good enough?" Her voice was now laced with concern. "If you can sit here and say he made you feel like you weren't good enough then you don't need to go back. Whether you love him or not."

"That's the only explanation as to why he's always cheating on me." I was convinced. What pissed me off the most was it wasn't like our sex life wasn't bomb as fuck. There wasn't anything I wasn't willing to try at least once for him.

"No, Ry, men cheat because we let them get away with it. Every time Quan cheated on you, what did you do?"

Beat him and her up, and then take him right back.

"You made it too easy for him to come back." She read my mind. "Fussing and fighting won't make a person respect you. That only gives them the upper hand." She schooled me. "Once someone has you so mad you're yelling at the top of your lungs or you're hitting on them, they have all the control over what matters the most."

I sat up. "And what's that?"

COVERED IN YOUR LOVE 2
by *Nique Luarks*

"Your peace of mind." She tapped her temple with her index finger. Standing up, she went into her closet. "If ever you get around someone and you can't find any peace, then you need to reevaluate the company you keep."

"That's the thing. With DaQuan the only time we have a fallout is when another woman is involved. Other than that, he is my peace." I looked down at my nails feeling overly emotional all of a sudden.

"Then work it out, Ryan." She came out of the closet to look at me. "You've been here for how long? Going on seven months? If he doesn't get it right this time around, he's not the one," she said sternly.

"And the baby?"

"Can you handle that?"

"No." I mumbled as a single tear slid down my right cheek.

"You can't want him, but not his child. Because if he's going to be a father, the baby will be around. Would you look at him like less of a man if he chose not to be involved in the baby's life if it meant he could have you back?"

Quan a deadbeat? Even though I hated Brianna, the thought alone was a turn off. Quan witnessed firsthand what it was like to not have a father. And it wasn't like his dad couldn't be there. He just didn't want to. When we were young, I used to listen to him vent about how angry he was at his dad. How he felt like he wasn't good enough.

Damn.

Life is a bitch.

"The look on your face answered my question." Lenora chuckled. "He's a package deal now."

I watched her disappear into her closet again. Falling onto back dramatically, I yawned. Even conversation seemed to tire me. Rubbing my eyes, I closed them and allowed what Lenora had said to resonate. I had the answer to my question, though.

Quan

I hadn't seen or talked to Brianna in nearly a week, so when I pulled up in front of my house and saw her car sitting in the driveway, I grimaced. Her presence annoyed the fuck out of me. I wished she would just stay the fuck away from me unless she had a doctor's appointment or she was going into labor. Hopping out of my whip, I closed the door and went for the trunk. I'd just left this boutique with Ava so she could help me pick some shit out for Ry.

I lifted my trunk the same time she got out of her car.

"We need to talk," she started immediately with the bullshit.

"Nah, *you* need to talk. I got shit to do." I pulled the bags out, making sure I had everything.

"Who is this for? You won't let me come in, but you letting a whole other bitch move in!" I'd told her ass time and time again about yelling in my face. "Or is Ryan's lovesick ass coming back? That bitch is dumb. You don't love nobody but yourself."

Closing the trunk, I sat the bags on top. It took me two steps to reach her and when I did, I wrapped my hands around her neck and lifted her into the air. "Bitch, you ain't been nothing but a muthafuckin' problem since day one."

COVERED IN YOUR LOVE 2
by *Nique Luarks*

Her legs dangled as she unsuccessfully tried to pry my hands from around her neck.

"You think I don't know you a hoe?" I growled, tightening my grip. "I'm the dumb ass for even fuckin' wit' yo slut ass."

She gagged. "Qua…qua…" Tears leaked from her eyes.

"I could kill you right here, right now if I wanted to and I'd get away with the shit." I dropped her and she hit the pavement gasping for air. Looking around, I made sure nobody was outside. It was almost midnight so most of my bougie-ass neighbors were sleep anyway.

"You…" She coughed, crying. "You could've killed me."

"I should've." I picked up the shopping bags. "Yo ass is trespassing."

"I can't do this no more." She bawled. "You ain't ever gon' love me."

I looked down at her looney ass as she rocked back and forth. "Yo, you trippin'. Take your pregnant ass home."

"It's not even worth it," She wailed. "All this heartache ain't even worth it." Snot bubbles hung from her nose.

"What the fuck are you talkin' about, B?"

My neighbor's porch light came on.

She wiped her nose with the sleeve of her jacket. "The baby…" she whimpered. "She's not yours."

My hand came down hard on her face, sending her flying sideways.

I'm bout to murk this bitch.

I pulled my piece from my waistband.

"Hey, what are you doing over there?"

I quickly stuck my burner in one of the bags. "Don't worry about what the fuck I'm doin' over here." I mugged a white man who was standing on his porch.

"What's all that screaming then? I'm going to call the police." He quickly turned around and disappeared back into his house.

Taking a deep breath, I picked the bags up with one hand. Brianna was still lying across the driveway crying her eyes out, telling me how much she hated me. I wanted to kick her ass, but I wasn't even built like that. Plus, I had something for her ass as soon as she dropped that baby. Bending down slightly so she could hear me clearly, I glared at her. "Get the fuck from around here, yo." Pulling her head back by her hair, I stared deep in her eyes. "I'ma kill you. Believe that. It just won't be today."

Her head dropped when I let go. "I'm sorry."

by *Nique Luarks*

"Not yet," I spoke over my shoulder.

Once I was in the house, I sat Ry's shit down and set the alarm. If Brianna was smart, she would move far the fuck away. I punched the wall in rage. That explained why her ass had disappeared. Since she was getting closer to her due date, the more I made it clear I wanted a DNA test, she'd been staying away from me.

I couldn't believe this shit. I'd wasted my time and damn near lost my mind, because I'd almost lost Ryan. *Almost*. I had to get my baby back. I had to prove to her that I could be better than I was.

Chapter Eighteen

...Please be love

Jaime

After her month-long stay, Jaylen was finally going back to Florida. I knew the day was coming soon, but I wasn't ready to let her go just yet. As I helped her and Maxx walk their luggage through the airport, my heart got heavy. Goodbyes were always hard for me. Deciding I would sulk in the car, I prepared to see my baby sister off.

"Maxxie, I sure am going to miss you," I spoke to my niece.

"I'ma miss you too, Auntie Meme," she pouted. "I'm glad Duke has a cell phone now, though."

I chuckled, thinking back on how she had saved her number underneath a bunch of emojis so Duke would know it was her calling.

"We're coming back for the summer," Jaylen promised. "I don't like being away that long."

"I'ma hold you to that. You hear that, Maxx?" I asked as we neared the boarding area.

"Yep." She smiled. "Uncle Nas said we're going to Disneyland anyway."

"This is it." Len grabbed the bags out of my hand. She held her arms out for a hug and I pulled her in and held her tight. "I love you, Meme. I'ma call you every day."

"I love you too. You know if you don't, I'll be calling you." I let her go to embrace Maxx.

"Bye, Auntie."

"Bye, Maxxie. I love you." Parting ways, I watched sadly as they went to catch their plane.

***

"What the hell?!" I shouted as Nas pulled up in front of my brownstone. I jumped out of the car before he could even come to a full stop. Tears burned in my eyes as I watched as people rummaged through what looked to be Duke's and my belongings.

"Stop." I cried.

"Jaime!" Nas hopped out of the car behind me.

"Put that down!" I tried to guard all of my shit. "No!" I cried as Nas pulled me into his arms.

"Baby, chill," Nas whispered in my ear. "Stop crying."

I watched with a blurred vision as people scurried off. I felt like I was having an out-of-body experience. All of our clothes and even the furniture were sitting on the sidewalk. Placing my face in Nas' chest, I bawled like a baby. Troy had done some lowdown, dirty shit, but this…*this* was fucked up.

He hadn't even thought about where Duke would live. He didn't care that strangers had taken more than half of his son's wardrobe. Nas rubbed my back as he talked to me.

"Baby, stop." He sighed. "All this shit can be replaced."

I cried harder.

"We can go get new shit right now if you want." He hugged me tighter. "Get in the car."

Where would we go?

This is so fucked up, yo.

I broke down again.

"Jaime…" He sounded the way I felt. Like I was losing control.

"He put his son out on the streets."

"He ain't put Duke on the streets and you either. He put ya'll shit out," he stressed, caressing my back.

"Why would he do that?" The cold air started drying the tears on my face.

"I got you, a'ight?" He cupped my face. "Look at me. Jaime." The sad look in his eyes resembled the same one he'd had at his mother's house when she'd mentioned his brother.

I sniffled.

"Stop crying, baby." He kissed me and then planted his forehead on mine. "I got ya'll." Wiping my tears away with his thumbs, he kissed me again.

Pulling away from him, I looked dolefully at the pile of clothes, shoes, furniture, pictures, and even food. Slowly walking to the computer stand that was once in my guest bedroom, I opened the drawer. Tears slid down my face as I removed my poem book. Thankfully, all my school work and my laptop was at Nas' house since we'd been there so much. I watched sadly as Nas picked up pictures of me and Duke.

Once we had everything that was valuable to me in Nas' G-Wagon, I took one last glance at my brownstone and hopped in the car. Shutting my door, I sunk into the seat. Nas started the car as I pulled my seatbelt across my body. As we drove away from my home, tears sprung from my eyes. Depression consumed me almost instantly.

The entire ride to Nas' house was a silent one. Even Duke hadn't uttered a word. My head was pounding and my eyes were sore from rubbing away tears. By the time we pulled into his wrap-a-around driveway, I was numb. Nas helped a sleeping Duke out the back seat and opened my door, but I didn't budge.

He stared at me intently.

Facing forward in my seat, I started crying again.

Nas shut my door back and took off with Duke into the house. Hanging my head, I felt so low. Low like when my mother passed, low like when my daddy blamed himself for her death and started using, low like when I found out Troy was married. I was literally drowning in my sorrows, losing myself, when Nas opened my door again. I knew I had to be strong for Duke, but I felt weak and helpless.

Nas turned me around in my seat. Wiping my face, he stared at me. "I love you."

I couldn't stop crying.

"You know why I love you?" He kissed my trembling lips.

Closing my eyes, I hung my head. What was there to love about me? I was a single mother, working on a degree with no job and now no home.

"You asked me how did I know you were selfless?" He whispered against my lips. "Because even though you've been through a bunch of bullshit, you still find time to keep a smile on Duke's face and mine too."

Even though my eyes were shut tight, warm tears slid down out of them and down my cheeks.

"Stop crying. I got ya'll. You and Duke. He aint gotta want for shit as long as I'm alive." He wiped my face. "Even when I'm dead and gone he gon' be straight."

I sniffled.

"I need you to stop crying, though, cause when you hurt, I hurt too."

Nas

I'd finally gotten Jaime in the house after standing in the cold for another ten or fifteen minutes. We took a shower and now, she was sleeping peacefully underneath me. I ain't ever been a emotional nigga, but seeing my lil' baby break down like that, had me feeling some type of way. It was taking everything in me not to fuck her baby daddy up. Duke didn't need a nigga like him in his life.

Jaime deserved anything and everything she asked for. She was too good of a person to have to deal with a fuck nigga. Shit, I even found myself switching up how I came at her from time to time. Jaime had me saying shit like *sorry*, and *are you okay*. In a short time, she and Duke had become the most important people in my life.

"Jaime." I kissed her forehead. "Wake up."

"Hmmm?" she mumbled.

Running my hand up her thigh and massaging her ass, I pulled her closer. "You ain't ever gotta worry about no shit like that happening ever again."

"Nas, I don't wanna talk about it." She turned her face.

"I'm dead ass."

"Okay." She sighed. "Nas?"

"What's up?"

"Did you really mean what you said outside?"

"Yeah."

"Good. Cause I love you too."

"Ah yeah?"

"Yeah."

"Why?" All my life the only love I'd received from women was from my family. I watched first-hand the shit love did to you and put you through. I never had time for a relationship and the headaches bitches came with. Wasn't shit loveable about me, but Jaime claimed she loved me. I wanted to know why.

"Because you never gave up on me even when I gave up on you. The way you look out for Duke like you fathered him is probably why I love you the most, though. You make me feel safe. And honestly, besides Duke, I feel like you're the only for-sure thing in my life." She sat up. "Just don't ever stop loving me, okay?"

"I got you."

***

"Nas, can you tell Duke to stop cussing?" Tati rounded the corner with Duke behind her driving his Maybach.

"Yo, Tati..." Cole shook his head. "Why you always snitchin'? I didn't raise you to be that way."

Kai Money chuckled.

"It ain't my fault he's bad." She hopped in her daddy's lap.

I'd been on Duke about his mouth all week. I was about to get to a point where I said fuck it. Jaime complained he was getting it from me, but shit, cursing was like a second language to me.

"Lil' Duke." Quan put the blunt out. "Let me hold a dollar."

"I ain't got no dollar." Duke stopped driving to do something on his iPad.

"You rolling around in a Maybach and yo pockets empty?" Quan shook his head. "You gotta do better, my guy."

"Tell that nigga not worry about what the fuck is in your pockets." I took a sip of the lean in my cup.

"Don't worry about what the fuck is in my pockets," Duke said, still looking down at his iPad

"Excuse you."

The sound of Jaime's voice made me look at the door. "What's up, baby?"

"Why do you have Duke in here cursing?" Blaze entered the room holding Kyre.

"Are ya'll really surprised?" Kenya stood at the entrance with Jaime. "Look who he's sitting around."

"That's what I said." Tati combed through her baby doll's head.

"You ain't said nothing." Cole tickled her sides.

Kai stood up and Blaze handed him Kyre. "Where's Kyra?" He started out of the room and she followed him.

"Sleep. She's been fussing all day."

"Tati, let's go." Kenya ushered. "You don't need to be sitting in here while they smoke." She watched Tati skip towards her. "You either, Duke."

Jaime nodded in agreement.

"I'm chillin'." Duke's iPad had his attention again.

Cole and Quan chuckled.

"No, he didn't." Kenya snickered, walking away.

"We bout to head out anyway," I said, standing up. Duke and I had been at Kai's house with the homies while the ladies went shopping. He and Jaime needed whole new wardrobes, so after a couple of days of moping around the crib, Blaze convinced her to get out the house.

"A'ight." Quan gave me dap.

"I'ma link up wit' you later." Cole hit me with a reverse nod.

"Bet."

Duke drove behind us as we left the room. "You get everything you need?" I asked Jaime.

"Yeah, more then I needed actually. Kenya can shop." She smiled, shaking her head.

"Duke straight?" I asked, already knowing the answer. Even before all that shit with her bitch-ass baby daddy, Duke had started accumulating clothes at my spot because I'd cop him something at the mall if I got me something.

"Yeah, he's straight." She opened the front door.

"Hop out, Duke." I helped him out of his whip. Picking it up, I shut the front door and carried it to the back of my whip. "Did you go take that jeep back like I told you too?" I asked Jaime as she helped Duke in his seat.

"No," she said lowly.

After making sure Duke's power wheel was straight, I shut the door. "Why the fuck not?"

"Ew..." Jaime frowned. Ignoring my question she got in the car and slammed her door.

Shaking my head, I hopped inside too. "What you ewing for?"

"Because you curse too much, and you don't know how to talk to people," she mumbled, scrolling through her Instagram timeline.

"Nah, you don't know how to listen." I'd told Jaime to have Kenya drop her off at the crib and follow her to drop the jeep off. My bitch wasn't driving nothing no other nigga had bought. I wasn't going out like that.

"I like my jeep. I just got it painted last summer."

"You can get another one and paint it a different color every day if you want." I stopped at the gate and waited for security to open it. "But you returning that muthafucka today," I finalized.

"Whatever." She looked out of her window.

"And we gon' have to find you a better word to use when you don't like something, because *ew* is corny as shit." I chuckled, looking over at her.

She pressed her lips together to keep from smiling.

Chapter Nineteen

The heart has to be broken, to open

Jaime

Nas pulled up behind me as I came to a stop in front of my old brownstone. I didn't want to return my jeep, but I also wasn't trying to hear his mouth about it anymore. Getting out, I sat the keys in the seat, locked the door and shut it. It wasn't my problem or my concern as to how Troy would get the keys out. I was walking to the passenger's side of Nas' car when I heard a door shut.

Looking up toward the front door to where I used to call home, Jade came sashaying down the stairs.

Wait...

I had to close my eyes and then open them again to make sure I wasn't tripping. Rage surged through my body as all the love I had for my sister started diminishing. Her eyes landed on mine and a shocked expression graced her face. With my fist balled up I took off in her direction, but before I could even get a good start, Nas had me in a bear hug. Jade stayed at the top of the stairs.

"You scandalous, lowdown, bum-ass bitch!" I screamed.

"Jaime..." Nas tried pulling me to the car.

"I'ma beat your ass, Jade. I swear to God!" I elbowed Nas hard. "Get the fuck off of me!"

"Calm your mothafuckin' ass down!" he roared angrily. "Hit me again," Nas warned.

"Jaime, you being real extra." Jade finally found her voice. "I told you Troy wasn't shit."

"And what the fuck are *you*, Jade?!" My voice cracked.

"You taking this shit personal." She had the nerve to catch an attitude.

"Personal?" I tried charging at her again.

"*Jaime*!" Nas grabbed the front of my jacket and spun me around. "What the fuck did I say? Fuck that dumb-ass bitch! You don't see Duke in this car?!" he yelled in my face.

At the mention of Duke's name, I came back down to reality. In *reality,* Jade was a grimy bitch. And in *reality* I already knew that. I just didn't think she could be so cold towards *me.* How could she be so heartless?

"Jaime, you got a man with money. Why is it fair that you get to have the best of both worlds?" Jade's stupidity was shining through.

"Nas, let me go. I'm good." I assured him. He was right. Duke didn't need to witness me acting a fool, especially not with his auntie. Plus, I'd beaten Jade's ass enough at the club.

"If you start buggin', I'ma drag yo ass by your hair back to the whip." Nas' face stayed hard. "And that's on my brother, son." He let me go.

I rolled my eyes. We were going to have to talk about how he talked to me. And we were having that conversation the minute we got home. Facing Jade, I sighed. This was just my luck.

Heartbreak was my life.

"Jade, it's taking everything in me not to hate you." I stared at my big sister. "I've known you my whole life and this is how you do me?"

"Meme, you gon' be straight either way." She huffed. "It ain't like you gon' miss Troy's money. You don't want nobody to win but you."

"How was I winning, Jade? Troy has a wife. He won't even claim his son in public. You've seen first-hand how hard it's been for me!" My voice rose unintentionally.

"But you got Nas now," she argued.

"So, you're staying here now? Is that why he put our shit on the curb!?" I was mad all over again.

"I told him you've been at Nas' house." She shrugged. "He stopped by one day looking for you and Duke it slipped out."

"And you knew he was going to put your nephew's shit out and you didn't think to tell me?"

"We weren't talking."

Wow

Officially done with Jade, I turned back around to get in the car. Family was supposed to be forever. At least that's what I thought. But I couldn't continue any kind of relationship with Jade. I was too scared to ask Jade if she and Troy were fucking, because if she said the wrong thing, I would've gladly ended her life with Nas' gun.

Nas opened my door and I got in. Jade continued to stand on the porch. The smug look on her face was almost enough for me to throw all caution to the wind and hop back out of the car. As Nas pulled away from curb, I sighed, shaking my head in disappointment. I was so overwhelmed that I couldn't even think straight.

How could she do that to me, her sister?

It wasn't like we were half-sisters or even sisters that didn't speak all the time. No, we had the same mother and father, we'd shared the same room growing up, and up until recently, I'd stupidly been her designated babysitter. So, yeah, my thoughts were jumbled. Picking my phone up, I got ready to text Jaylen.

"You bet not call that nigga." Nas who'd stopped at stop sign was looking down at his own phone.

"I'm not." I knew he was referring to Troy. Little did he know, I didn't have shit to discuss with Troy Warren. He'd been nothing but grief since I'd met him, and I was more than happy to be rid of him for good. I still hadn't spoken to him and he hadn't even called Duke's phone.

Nas nodded. "What you wanna eat, Duke?" He looked at the rearview mirror.

"Uhhh.. I don't know. Mama, what you want?" Duke asked me sweetly.

"Whatever you want, Bean." I pulled up the texts between Len and me.

Me: Your sister is dead to me.

by *Nique Luarks*

Ryan

I'd just left Summit Grill for their famous macaroni and cheese and I couldn't wait to get home and devour it. I'd been on a mac and cheese kick for about week now. Well, cheese period. I was low-key celebrating me officially being done with school. I didn't get a bachelor's or no shit like that, but I was proud of my accomplishment. This was simply a stepping stone for me. Life could only get better from here.

It has to.

I dug in the bag for one of the mozzarella sticks I'd bought at Sonics. Ms. Lenora's joke about me turning into a mozzarella stick ran through my mind.

That lady…

She'd slowly become my confident. Her words of wisdom had helped me get through some of my darkest days. She didn't judge me and she let me be me. She understood I was a little rough around the edges, and some days, I just didn't wanna be bothered. Ms. Lenora was my nigga.

That's why I was going to miss her. Since I'd spoken to the girls, Blaze's offer made me realize I didn't have to run away from home to live a happy, successful life. Blaze was talented as fuck and only worked with the best, so I knew I had a real chance of doing something productive and proactive with my life. The only pressing issue was Quan. The dude wouldn't let up.

Every other day, I was getting a letter or a package. I'd accumulated so much jewelry, perfumes, purses, and shoes that it was *crazy*. I was still ignoring him, though, no matter how much I still missed him. I was learning the first step to getting over heartbreak was working on yourself and I was doing just that. Quan had other responsibilities, and I didn't want anything to do with that.

My phone started going off, and I answered on the dashboard. "What's up?"

"*Congratulations!*" Ava, Kenya, and Blaze shouted.

I cheesed.

"We're so proud of you, Ry," Blaze cooed.

"I'm taking a shot for you now," Ava said and then told somebody to move.

"You know we're turning up!" Kenya added. "Cole said congrats."

"Thank you, everybody." I bit down on another mozzarella stick.

"What are you doing?"

I'm sure they thought I was out having a drink or something, but I wasn't even in that mind frame. I wanted to chill and celebrate my milestone and eat my macaroni. "I'm going to the house to chill. I'm not even in a drinking mood."

"Bitch, you pregnant!" Ava's loud ass made me turn the volume down.

"Ava, bitch…really?" Kenya smacked her lips. "Are you purposely trying to burst eardrums?"

"Ry, you pregnant?" Ava asked, ignoring Kenya.

"No." I shook my head. All the sex me and Quan had it never happened, so I was almost positive that wasn't possible. "I'm just coolin'. Is that alright with you?"

"Yeah. A'ight, hoe. Let me find out," Ava pressed.

"Well, were about to go shopping. We just wanted to call you and tell you we're proud of you." I could hear the smile in Blaze's voice.

"Ya'll know what size I wear," I joked—*a little*.

"Later." They all said in unison.

Pulling into the driveway, I put my ride in park and took the keys out of the ignition. Making sure I had everything, I got out, hitting the lock on the key fob. The spiked Louboutin's on my feet gifted by Quan, clicked loudly against the concrete as I tried to speed walk towards the door and out of the rain. I smiled inwardly. I loved the rain.

It was the perfect weather to spark up a blunt, turn on some neo-soul, and practice my craft.

Maybe that's what I'll do.

Unlocking the front door, I pushed my way into the darkness and shut the door back. Kenya and her damn black out curtains made me trip over one of my shoes in the hallway. Cursing quietly to myself, I ran my hand across the wall to find the switch. Finally finding it, I smelled a familiar scent. The butterflies in my stomach made me nervous to flip the switch, but when I did I almost jumped out of my skin.

Chapter 20

Infinite love

Quan

"Surprise!" Ava, Blaze, and Kenya yelled, rushing towards Ry.

She grinned as they all hugged on her. "What are ya'll doing here!" She laughed, shaking her head.

"We celebrating, bitch! Fuck what you talking about." Ava handed her a champagne flute. "The whole gang is here."

She looked further into the living room. Kai and Cole were lounging around and Nas had Jaime in his lap. "Wow." Ry laughed. "I feel so special," he joked.

"Cause you are." I licked my lips eyeing her, but she wouldn't even look at me.

"Congratulations, Ryan." Jaime smiled.

"You know the family had to come show you some love." Nas wrapped his arms around her waist.

"That's what's up." I could definitely feel the love in the room.

by *Nique Luarks*

"You can't look at me, Ry? It's like that?" She turned on her heels to face me.

Pretty ass.

"What's up Quan?" She hit a nigga with the head nod.

"You got me fucked up." I approached her as she sat all her shit down on the table.

"We didn't invite him," Ava's hating ass chimed in.

Grabbing Ry from the back, I hugged her. I kissed her tattoo than licked her earlobe. "I'm proud of you, baby," I whispered.

She shivered. "Can you get off me?" she asked dryly.

"You really ain't fuckin' wit ya boy, huh?" I held on tighter.

"Come on. Let's give them some privacy." Blaze pulled Kai Money by his arm.

"Nah." I shook my head. "Ya'll fam so ya'll straight."

Ry tried to wiggle free. "DaQuan, for real…"

"Chill out."I pulled her in closer. Her ass sat on my dick making me brick up. "I love you, Ry. I wanna be wit' you, Ma. I know I fucked up in the past. Shit, I'ma fucked up nigga." I shook my head. I was disappointed and disgusted in my own self. Ryan had always been too good for me.

"And I know you probably won't believe me when I say I'ma changed nigga."

"Shit, I know I don't." Ava sipped loudly from her glass.

"Shut up!" Nas shook his head.

"I don't wanna live without you, man. Whatever you want me to do to make this shit right, just tell me." I begged. "Brianna is out of the picture, so ain't no baby." A real nigga was on the verge of tears in front of the homies.

Ryan turned around to face me with a confused expression. "What you mean there ain't no baby?"

"It wasn't mine. I was pressuring her about a DNA test and the bitch did even wanna take it. Ended up telling me it wasn't even mine."

"I knew it. Trifling-ass bitch." Ava smacked her lips. "Quan the dumb ass that fell for the okey-doke."

"Ava…" Kai Money glared at her.

"I'm bout to put her ass outside in the rain." I looked at her and she rolled her eyes at me.

"I wish you would," she mumbled, taking a seat on the sofa next to Kenya.

"So, you think that's going to change the fact you stay cheating on me?"

"Nah, it won't change that." I licked my lips. "But I can change." I stared in her eyes. "That's why I wanted my boys here.

by *Nique Luarks*

So, everybody could see I wanna do right by you, Ry." He went in his pocket and pulled out a red velvet box.

Kenya squealed.

"Baby, let me show you how much I love you. We ain't even gotta stay in New York, yo. Wherever you go, I'ma follow you. I know you love me too, My Ry." Her eyes watered. "And I know a nigga gotta earn yo trust back and I'm down to do that too. No passwords on my phones, no late nights, no nothing."

"Quan..." She sighed.

"Ry, don't give up on us, man." I could see the doubt in her eyes. She didn't believe a word I was saying. "Just tell me what I gotta do." I stared at her intently. "Just say the word, yo." I sighed. This wasn't going like I had planned. Call me dumb, but I thought we had a real chance at making shit work between us.

"Get on your knees and ask." She stared back at me.

"What?"

"You heard her, nigga." Ava was smiling.

Shaking my head slowly, I ran my tongue across my top row of teeth. Saying fuck my pride, I got down on one knee and grabbed her hand. "My Ry, will you marry me?" I held my breath in.

"No." She pulled her hand away.

What?

"Ah damn, that's cold." Nas chuckled.

"No?" I had to make sure I had heard her ass right.

"No," she repeated. "If I accept that ring from you it has to be your promise to me, DaQuan. Your promise to be better, and stay true to everything you just said."

I nodded.

"The first time you fuck up, you won't ever hear from me again." Her eyes bore into me. "DaQuan, I swear on my grandmother's grave this is it." She took the velvet box from me. "I want your number changed, I want a new house, I want a new car, and I want a puppy."

"Done."

She slipped the ring on and I stood up. "This doesn't mean everything goes back to how it was. You said you were willing to earn my trust."

"I am." I pulled her close. "Whatever it takes." Placing my forehead on hers, I stared into her eyes.

"You got one time, Quan, even if I feel like you're on some bullshit," she warned me, gazing at me.

"I only want you." I promised.

"Can ya'll kiss and make up now?" Ava started again. "Ya'll making my stomach hurt with all this mushy shit."

Grabbing the sides of Ry's face, I planted a soft kiss on her lips.

Three days later...

Ryan

"I'm going to miss you." Ms. Lenora hugged me tight.

"I'ma miss you too." I sighed sadly.

"You're going to send for me, right? I'll have my own room in one of those big rooms, right?" She let me go.

"You know you will."

Ms. Lenora swiped her tears away. "I'm proud of you, Ryan. Make sure you keep in touch, okay?"

"Okay." I nodded.

"And if you ever need to borrow some sugar, you have my number.

I chuckled.

"And Ryan..." She looked me dead in the eyes. "Never settle."

"I won't."

Taking one more look at her, I left off of her porch and started to my car. Opening my door, I got in. I didn't realize how much of a bond we'd built. Quickly blinking away my tears, I started my car. Picking up the blunt in my ash tray, I lit it and pulled off.

"You straight?" Quan asked, leaning back in his seat.

"Yeah." I nodded, chilling in my own seat. Ms. Lenora was like the fairy godmother all girls needed.

"So, that's ole boy's mama?" he asked, taking the joint from me.

"Yeah."

"You fuck him recently?"

"Quan, really? Why does that even matter?" I rolled my eyes.

"It don't matter." He shook his head. "I should've killed that nigga." He sneered, hitting the weed.

"And I should've killed you *and* that bitch," I spat back.

"So, you saying we even?" He chuckled, passing the blunt back.

I shook my head slowly from side to side. "Not even close. I should've been done wit' your ass a long time ago." I flipped my turn signal and switched lanes.

"You should've, but we were made for each other."

"Meaning?"

"*Meaning…*" He mocked me and I snickered. "The love you got for me is deep. That's why I believe you when you said this is my last chance. You done already gave me too many free passes."

I took a toke of the weed.

"I'ma real nigga, so I can address my fuck-ups. I don't ever wanna be away from you again." He slid his hand up my thigh.

"Then you gotta do right by me, Quan." I put the weed out and cracked the windows.

"I know."

I handed him a piece of gum and popped a piece in my own mouth.

"And I will."

Chapter Twenty-One

Sometime in the middle of April…

Ryan

"Ry, can I have this?" Ava asked, holding up a Fenty eye shadow palette.

"I don't care." I shrugged.

"Bitch, ain't you supposed to be helping?" Kenya poked her head out of the closet.

"I am helping." Ava began testing the different shades.

"No, you're not." Blaze giggled, handing Jaime the blunt.

We were all sitting in the master bedroom of my new home. Staying true to his word, Quan had bought a house in Jersey close to Kenya and Cole. We'd just gotten the keys a few days ago and the ladies had agreed to help me unpack. We'd been together since early in the morning and it was now going on eight at night. We'd made a lot of progress even though Ava had disappeared a few times.

Jaime stood up to stretch. "Nas said the guys are on their ways to do pickups." She snickered. Probably laughing at some inside joke between her and bro. They were always laughing and flirting.

I smiled.

"Good cause I'm hungry." Kenya rubbed her protruding belly. "I'm telling Cole ya'll starved me." She was going into her fifth month of pregnancy.

"And then you'll be lying." Blaze stood up.

"Right. Don't be having Cole come up in here trippin'." I followed suit, fixing the waistband of my PINK tights.

"Greedy ass." Ava dropped the palette into her purse. "Minus Kenya, ya'll wanna go have drinks?"

"Nah, Quan and me are going out to eat and to the movies." I picked my puppy up. She was a *West Highland Terrier* and I loved her little ass to pieces.

"What about ya'll?" She looked to Blaze and Jaime.

"Can't." Blaze shrugged. "Mehkai and I have to be up early in the morning. Remember?" she asked, making sure she had everything.

"That's dope that he goes and sits in on your therapy sessions with you sometimes." Jaime passed the weed to me.

"I know right." Blaze blushed. A few times out of the month, Blaze flew to Missouri to sit with a therapist, her mother, and her father, to discuss her mother's absence. Kai Money would go once a month when it was just her and the therapist to make sure she was okay.

"Uh…okaaaay," Ava drawled. "What about you, Jaime?"

Jaime fake pouted. "Nas said he has something he wants to show me. I'll still see you Wednesday, though, right?" It was mad crazy she and Ava went from hitting each other with liquor bottles, to damn near being besties.

"Ugh, you bitches are sad." She led the way out of the bedroom. "I swear I don't wanna end up like ya'll miserable bitches."

I laughed. "Why we gotta be miserable?"

She sucked her teeth. "Ain't that much happiness in the world."

"You just haven't found your soul mate yet, Ava." Blaze took Fergie out of my arms as we all descended the glass staircase.

"And I never will."

"Never say never." Kenya chuckled.

"Exactly," Jaime said. "Love kind of just comes out of nowhere."

"You hoes are too soft for me." She shook her head. "Ugh. I need some new home girls. Bitches can't even stay out past midnight."

We all shared a hearty laugh as we reached the landing.

"Ava, when you fall in love, you gon' fall hard. Watch." I smirked. Ava talked the most shit about love and relationships because she ran from it. Whenever a man got to close to her, she'd push him away.

"Only thing I'm falling on is dick." She grinned.

"Hoe shit…" Quan came from the back of the house.

I smiled. "Hey, baby." That must've meant everyone's ride was present.

"What's up, My Ry…" He pulled me into a hug and kissed behind my ear. "I missed you today."

"I missed you too, baby." I kissed his lips.

"Ugh." Ava sashayed towards the front door with Kenya, Jaime, and Blaze following close behind.

Wrapping my arm around his neck, I gazed into his eyes. Everything I needed was right here with Quan. At first I had my doubts, but every day he proved to me he was trying. No late nights, and he answered every time I called. Most people would call me dumb for taking Quan back, but we had a connection *most* people couldn't relate to.

Now, I wasn't a fool. I knew nothing in life was perfect. Every relationship had its trials and tribulations. When the amount of love you have for a person is challenged, it's up to you to decipher whether or not it's worth the fight. Me and Quan, though. We have a tough love and I'm going to war for mine.

Jaime

"Why are we here?" I asked, staring out of my window.

"Just hop out the whip." He sighed, shaking his head.

Pushing the door open, I stepped into the night air. The wind blew past my face, sending my long hair sailing backwards. Shutting the door, I met Nas at the hood of his car. Taking his hand we walked to my favorite spot. Once we stopped, he looked up at the night sky.

"We missed the sunset." I wrapped my arms around his waist.

"I know." He kissed my forehead. "This is better, though." He spoke low, still gazing upward.

"How so? It's dark." I stared at the side of his face.

"Because the stars come out when the sun goes down." He shrugged nonchalantly.

I laid my head on his side.

"You know in your poem when you were like, you just wanna see the light at the end of the tunnel?"

He remembers.

"Yeah." I held him tighter.

"I was thinking we could be that for each other. That light."
I could tell he was having a hard time getting his words out.

Butterflies swarmed in my abdomen. He remembered my poem.

"So, yeah, the sunset is dope, but even it ain't nothing but a star." He licked his lips. "Yo, Jaime, I ain't tryna be no sap-ass nigga; but you my sunrise, my sunset, and starry night."

I blushed.

"I ain't ever going nowhere." He looked down at me.

"I love you Nas." I gazed into his eyes. Moments like these I would cherish forever. Before him, my life seemed to be wrapped up into one big ball of chaos; feeling worthless during the day, and lonely at night. Now, I had somebody who knew I was flawed and in his eyes, I was still a star. My heart swelled.

"I love you too."

THE END

Want to be notified when the new, hot Urban Fiction and Interracial Romance books are released? Text the keyword "JWP" to 22828 to receive an email notifying you of new releases, giveaways, announcements, and more!

Jessica Watkins Presents is currently accepting submissions for the following genres: Urban Romance, Interracial Romance, and Interracial Romance/Paranormal. If you are interested in becoming a best selling author and have a complete manuscript, please send the synopsis and the first three chapters to jwp.submissions@gmail.com.